# ALIAS THE GHOST

Some dark and sinister mystery surrounds wealthy financier Milton Vaizey, who has taken extensive security precautions to guard the grounds of his house. Despite these, however, his secretary is shot dead through the window by a rifleman hidden outside — is this the nameless adversary whom Vaizey fears? Investigating police officer Superintendent Bill Groom is convinced that it is. And then Vaizey himself is murdered . . . Who is the killer? What is the motive for both deaths? And how are they linked to the elusive blackmailer known only as The Ghost?

# GERALD VERNER

---

# ALIAS
# THE GHOST

*Complete and Unabridged*

# LINFORD
*Leicester*

First published in Great Britain

First Linford Edition
published 2016

A catalogue record for this book is available
from the British Library.

ISBN 978–1–4448–2881–8

# 1

## The Tragedy at the Priory

It was a night of storm and rain; a night when it is pleasant to gaze out upon the streaming and splattered streets from within the sanctuary of a warm room and be thankful that one is not abroad. A night when the cheerful crackling of a fire becomes almost one of the chief pleasures of life, and the sound of the rain rattling on the window panes and the howling of the wind causes one to draw their chair closer to the leaping flames, and in slippered ease think regretfully of the people whose business necessitates their being out in such inclement weather.

All day the wind had been rising steadily, and with the approach of nightfall had increased to such violence that it was now blowing with almost the force of a gale. It shrieked and whistled round the walls and chimneys of mansions and cottages, farms and homesteads, and swept across the open country in great boisterous gusts, causing the leafless trees to bow their heads before its tempestuous advance, and sending the wrack of rain clouds scurrying across the pale face of the watery moon in their hurry to escape from its pursuit.

It lashed the rain into a fury, dashing it against the glass screen of Superintendent William Groom's powerful car, as it sped along one of the narrow roads crossing Oxshott Heath, and made the drops swirl and dance in the rays of the brilliant headlights. Driving was difficult on such a night, for in spite of the automatic wiper, the glass was so blurred that it caused a distortion of vision, and made it almost impossible to see further than a few yards beyond the long radiator.

On the more frequented roads, Groom had been forced, in consequence, to proceed at almost a crawl; but here, where there was no likelihood of meeting any traffic at that hour of the night — for it was approaching eleven o'clock — he was able to increase the speed with comparative safety.

'What a beastly night, Bill,' said his companion, Charlie Stephens, more popularly known as Bluey, on account of the fact that he was usually smeared with some of the blue-black fluid manufactured by his namesake. 'I shall be glad to see home and a warm fire.'

'So shall I, Bluey,' agreed Groom. 'If I'd thought it was going to turn out as bad as this, I'd have postponed our visit.'

The young superintendent of police and his friend, a reporter on the *Daily Messenger*, had taken advantage of a slack day — a rarity seldom enjoyed in either of their adventurous professions — to pay a long-delayed visit to an old friend of Groom's in the country.

It had been dry when they had left London early that afternoon, and it was not until they were approaching their destination that the rain had started. It was merely a fine drizzle at first, but had rapidly developed into a heavy downpour that had not ceased all through the evening.

Sir Bryan Walsh, the well-known scientist, whom Groom had been to see, lived in a large house just outside Stoke D'Abernon, and he had tried to persuade them both to stay the night; but Groom and Stephens had work to do early the following morning, and were obliged to refuse the invitation.

The wheels of the car slipped and skidded over the streaming surface of the road they were traversing as Bill pressed his foot gently on the accelerator and allowed the machine to travel as fast as he dared. Presently they left the heath and swung onto the Oxshott Road. Here the wind was less violent, its noisy blasts being checked somewhat by the surrounding trees and high hedges. They drove on in silence; Stephens was feeling too tired to talk, and Bill Groom's entire attention was concentrated on the car. He sat rigidly behind the wheel, his eyes straining to pierce the watery mist that obscured the windscreen. They were nearing the outskirts of Esher when suddenly, during a lull following a particularly heavy gust of wind, a sound was borne to their ears, clear and distinct. The sound of a shot!

Instinctively Groom brought the car to a standstill. 'Did you hear that, Bluey?' he asked sharply.

'Yes, old chap,' replied his friend. 'It sounded like a pistol shot.'

'It was undoubtedly a shot,' answered Groom, 'but it was not fired from a pistol. It came from a rifle, unless I'm greatly mistaken.'

'What on earth could anyone be doing with a rifle on a night like this?' exclaimed Bluey.

'I don't know,' answered Bill. 'It was certainly fired from quite close at hand. I think we ought to go and see if we can discover the reason. Some crime may have been committed or attempted.'

He opened the door near the driver's seat and stepped out into the rain. As he did so, he encountered the full force of the wind as a fresh squall whistled past the standing car. It almost threw him off his balance, and he had to retain his grip of the door to keep his feet. Waiting until it had died down, Groom walked round the back of the car and joined Bluey just as the boy — for he was little more — descended into the roadway.

'The shot came from somewhere over there,' he said, pointing across the dark road to where a high wall loomed out of the gloom, faintly visible in the reflected light from the car's powerful headlamps.

'It looks as if it encloses the grounds of some private house,' said Groom, taking an electric torch from his pocket and directing a circle of light on the shining brickwork. 'If so, I should think the entrance must be further on down the road.' He turned and retraced his steps to the waiting car.

'What are you going to do?' asked Stephens as he followed.

'Drive slowly on and see if we can find it,' answered Groom, taking his place behind the wheel. 'We don't know how far these grounds extend. It may be for a considerable distance, and I don't fancy walking far in this confounded rain. Besides, we can't leave the car here unattended.'

He sent the big car crawling forward,

while Stephens scanned the roadside for some sign of a break in the wall. They had proceeded for nearly two hundred yards when he saw that which they were seeking. 'Here you are, Bill,' he cried, and Groom again brought the car to a halt.

Almost opposite them, the high wall had taken a sudden crescent-shaped curve inwards, and in the centre of the semicircle thus formed was a massive iron gate set between two stone pillars, evidently the entrance to a drive. It was half-open, and Groom backed the car a few yards up the road they had come.

'Slip out and open the gate wide, Bluey,' he said, and Stephens hastened to obey.

As he approached the entrance, he glanced up at the stone pillars flanking the gate. Groom had turned the radiator of the car half-round towards it, preparatory to driving through, and the headlights shining full upon the pillars enabled the reporter to make out the name carved in the weather-beaten stone: The Priory. He opened the gate, securing it from being blown shut again by fastening it to an iron stanchion in the ground provided for that purpose, and got back into the car.

As they sped up the well-kept drive, Groom peered ahead, searching for some sign of a habitation, but without result. Beyond the range of the car's lamps, nothing was visible but black and impenetrable darkness. Suddenly the drive took a sharp bend to the right, and the superintendent saw, a short distance ahead, the bulk of a large grey house rising out of the mass of trees which grew thickly about it. A few seconds later he stopped the car at the foot of a flight of broad stone steps that led up to a wide portico.

He alighted and was in the act of ascending the steps when the door at the top was thrown open, and a man appeared on the threshold, silhouetted against a flood of orange light that came from a big hanging lamp in the hall behind him.

'Who's there?' cried a voice, and Bill Groom detected a note of agitation and fear in its tone. 'What do you want?'

The speaker was a short, stout man with a large, fat face and a bald head. His eyes were small and set close to a tremendous hook nose that seemed to be out of all proportion to the rest of his features. He peered at Groom as the superintendent reached him and blinked rapidly, as though he were staring at the glare of some strong light.

'Who are you?' he repeated. 'You can't be the police! They couldn't have had time to get here yet.'

'I was passing in my car,' explained Groom, 'and I heard the sound of a shot. It seemed to come from the grounds of this house. Has anything happened here? I'm Superintendent Groom of Scotland Yard.'

The short man caught him by the arm excitedly. 'Groom!' he exclaimed. 'Not the man who caught the Finsbury Park murderer — !'

Bill smiled. 'So you remember that, do you?' he said, recalling to his mind for a moment the case upon which he had sprung into prominence.

'Come inside, Mr. Groom,' said the

other quickly, and, still keeping a grip on Bill's arm, led him toward the lighted hall. Groom shot a keen glance round as, followed by Stephens, they crossed the threshold.

In the shadow of a broad staircase a group of frightened servants was huddled together, whispering excitedly, and Groom heard the sound of a stifled half-hysterical sob. Evidently something had taken place to throw the household into a state of agitation that was almost bordering on panic.

'My name is Vaizey — Milton Vaizey,' continued the short man after he had closed the main door. 'Perhaps you have heard of me?'

Groom nodded. The name of Milton Vaizey was well-known in the City. He was a financier, and his occasional spectacular coups on the stock exchange had more than once created a crisis in the financial world, among the men whose business it was to gamble in stocks and shares.

'It's a remarkable coincidence that you should be here, Mr. Groom,' Vaizey went on. 'A terrible thing has occurred. My secretary has been murdered!'

'Murdered!' echoed Groom sharply.

'Yes — shot in the library a few minutes ago,' answered Vaizey hoarsely. 'It's a ghastly business.'

'But the shot we heard was somewhere outside,' exclaimed Groom.

'Yes, yes, I know,' said Vaizey. 'She was shot from outside — through the window!' His voice shook, and he clasped and unclasped his podgy hands nervously while his small eyes blinked more rapidly than before. It was obvious that he was suffering from a severe shock.

'Are you quite sure she's dead?' asked Groom.

'The bullet passed through her head,' answered the short man. 'Of course, I haven't made a close examination. I was afraid to touch anything. My butler is phoning for the police now. I was waiting until they arrived.'

'In the meanwhile,' said Groom, 'if she is only wounded, the delay may prove fatal. I know something of first aid, Mr. Vaizey, so I think it would be as well if I saw her at once.'

'I shall be only too glad,' agreed Vaizey. 'I would rather the responsibility of this dreadful affair should be taken off my hands. Come this way, Mr. Groom.'

They crossed the hall, followed by the curious eyes of the servants, and ascended the wide staircase. Vaizey led the way along a corridor that evidently stretched towards the back of the house. There were several doors on either side, and from one of these, a door near the end on the left, a man emerged as they approached. He was dressed in the conventional garb of an upper servant, and Groom guessed that this was the butler whom Vaizey had mentioned. His face was white and his hands trembled slightly. As he caught sight of Groom and his friend, he stared in astonishment.

'Did you get through, Payne?' asked Vaizey as they drew level with him.

'Yes, sir,' answered the butler in a strained voice. 'Inspector Browne is coming up at once.'

'This is Superintendent Groom of Scotland Yard,' said Vaizey. 'Luckily he happened to be passing and heard the shot.'

Payne bowed his grey head. 'If you won't be wanting me, sir,' he said respectfully, 'I'll go and try and pacify the women servants. They are naturally rather upset.'

'I should like to have a word with you presently, Payne,' said Groom, 'but not at the moment.'

Payne bowed again and passed on down the corridors towards the stairs. Vaizey went to the door of the room from which the butler had recently emerged and, turning the handle, opened it gently. 'It happened in — in here,' he said in a low voice.

Groom stepped to his side and paused on the threshold for a moment, allowing his eyes to travel round the comfortably furnished room. It was a large apartment, and evidently more the workroom of a businessman than the library of a student. There were few books, the main furnishings consisting of filing cabinets, shelves filled with black japanned deed boxes, and other office equipment.

A large safe occupied one corner; and in the centre of the room, exactly opposite the window, was a big flat-topped writing table crowded with books and papers, on which stood a green-shaded reading lamp, the sole means of illumination that the room boasted. On the floor beside the table, face downwards and ominously still, lay the figure of a woman.

Groom took in the general details of the room in one swift, comprehensive glance, and then, crossing quickly to the writing table, bent down over the silent figure on the floor and gently turned it over so that the face was visible. It only needed one look to assure him that she was beyond human aid.

'I'm afraid she's quite dead,' he said gravely, looking up towards the door, where Vaizey still remained, visibly ill at ease.

'I feared as much,' the stout man replied shakily. Drawing a handkerchief from his pocket, he wiped off the drops of perspiration that beaded his forehead.

Groom dropped onto one knee beside

the body and commenced a close examination. The dead woman was middle-aged, and her face was almost masculine in its austere lines. Her hair was Eton-cropped; and this, together with the fact that she was dressed in a severe tailor-made costume of some dark material and wore a soft collar and tie, caused Groom almost to believe for a moment that it was a man, and not a woman at all, that lay there.

The bullet had struck her at the base of the skull and, penetrating the brain, passed out just above the left temple. She must have been killed instantly. There was nothing much to be learned from the body, and in a few seconds Groom rose to his feet and turned his attention to the window. A round hole in the glass near the bottom of the lower pane showed where the bullet had entered. After a brief scrutiny Bill returned to the writing table, his eyes fixed thoughtfully on the opposite wall.

'The bullet should be somewhere in there,' he said to Stephens, nodding in the direction of the wall. 'See if you can find it, Bluey. It will be fairly high up and almost in a line with the centre of this table.'

Bluey, who had been watching Groom's investigations with interest, hastened to obey. 'Here it is, Bill,' he said almost immediately, pointing to a spot in the middle of the wall some three feet above his head.

'Get your knife and prise it out,' said Groom a trifle absently, his fingers drumming gently on the polished corner of the table.

Stephens climbed up on a chair and, taking a penknife from his pocket, began to probe the plaster. The bullet had embedded itself in the woodwork behind, but after a few moments of digging he succeeded in extracting it. He sprang down from the chair and, crossing to Groom's side, dropped the little blob of metal into his friend's outstretched palm.

Groom held it under the light of the reading lamp and turned it over with a long forefinger. 'It's obviously a rifle bullet,' he remarked. 'Fired from a Lee-Enfield, I should imagine.' He slipped the bullet into his pocket and turned to Milton Vaizey. 'What was your secretary's name?' he asked.

'Bingham,' answered Vaizey. 'Elsa Bingham.'

'Was she married, or single?' Groom continued.

'Single, as far as I know,' said Vaizey.

'How long had she been in your employ?'

Vaizey thought for a moment. 'About eighteen months,' he replied.

'Have you any idea why she was killed, or who could have been responsible?' Groom watched the stout man closely as he put the question to him.

Vaizey shook his head emphatically. 'No, it's a complete mystery to me,' he declared.

'Was anyone with her when she met her death?' continued Groom.

'No, she was quite alone.'

'Who first made the discovery?'

'Payne and I together,' replied Vaizey. 'We were talking in the dining room, which is immediately under this room, when we heard the shot. It was followed instantly by a thud, which seemed to come from above. We both rushed upstairs at once and found Miss Bingham as you see her now.'

'Did the shot sound near or far away?' asked Groom.

'It was very clear and distinct,' answered Vaizey. 'I should think it was quite near.'

'Do you know anything about Miss Bingham's private life — her relations or friends, for instance?'

'No, nothing at all,' said Vaizey. 'She was very reserved about herself. I don't think she had any living relatives of any description. I always understood that she was an orphan.'

Groom paused for some seconds before putting his next question, his brows knitted in a puzzled frown. 'You are sure,' he said at length, 'that you can think of nothing? No trivial incident that happened, or remark that she may have dropped, that would be likely to form a clue to the person who shot her?'

'Nothing,' replied Vaizey. 'She seldom spoke to me except in connection with her work, and never mentioned anything about her private affairs.'

'Humph,' said Groom. 'There must have been a very strong motive behind her death, and until we can get some sort of clue as to what it was, we are working rather in the dark. I think the next step is to find the place from where the shot was actually fired. We may discover some traces there that will lead us to the identity of the murderer. How can I get out into the grounds?'

'There's a door at the end of the hall,' answered Vaizey. 'I'll show you.' He seemed anxious to leave the room of death, for he welcomed the excuse and stepped eagerly into the corridor.

'One moment,' said Bill. He moved the green-shaded reading lamp onto the blotting pad until it was directly in line with the chair the dead woman had been occupying when the bullet had so suddenly cut short her life. 'Now if you will show me the way,' he said, and joined Bluey in the corridor, closing and locking the library door behind him.

'I'll keep this key, if you don't mind,' said Groom as they made their way to the head of the staircase.

The little group of servants had disappeared when they reached the hall, but Payne was there, and Milton Vaizey called to him with an air of relief. 'Payne,' he said, 'Mr. Groom wants to find the way out into the grounds. Will you show him? I hope you'll excuse me,' he added to Bill, 'but I feel in need of some sort of restorative. This affair has completely upset my nerves. I'll be in the dining room if you want me for anything.'

Groom nodded and passed through a door on the left. As he followed the grey-haired butler, he heard the faint clink of glass upon glass proceeding from the room Vaizey had just entered, and his firm mouth curved into a quiet smile.

The butler led the way to a door set in a small alcove at the end of the hall. Here he paused. 'Are you thinking of going out into the grounds, sir?' he asked.

'That was my intention,' answered Groom.

'Then if you'll excuse me while I get my hat and coat,' said Payne. 'I'll come with you, if you don't mind, sir.'

'There's no need to do that,' said Bill. 'We can find our way quite easily.'

'I wasn't thinking of that, sir,' answered the butler. 'But it would be safer if I came with you.'

'Safer!' exclaimed Groom in surprise. 'Why?'

'Well, sir . . . ' Payne hesitated for the fraction of a second. 'The grounds are full of man-traps and tripwires, and as you are a stranger here, sir, you wouldn't be able to find your way among them in the dark.'

'Man-traps and tripwires!' echoed Bill in surprise. 'What are they there for?'

'The wires connect with alarm bells in the house. Mr. Vaizey is very nervous about burglars, sir,' explained Payne. 'He had the security features put down some months ago. I will not be a moment, sir.' He hurried away down a flight of stairs that led from the alcove to somewhere below.

Bluey looked quickly at Groom. His friend's usually smiling face was expressionless, but in the depths of his blue eyes lurked a little gleam — a gleam that

Stephens knew well, for it betokened intense interest. 'Well, Bill, what do you make of it?' he asked.

'It's an interesting problem,' murmured Groom. 'Very interesting. And the most interesting part of the whole affair is, of whom or of what is Milton Vaizey scared?'

'Scared,' echoed the reporter. 'What do you mean?'

Bill Groom made no reply. He was thinking deeply, for in Milton Vaizey's eyes he had seen the fear of death!

# 2

## A Shred of Blood-Stained Leather

Stephens was on the point of bursting into a string of questions, when the return of the butler forced him to remain silent. Payne was clad in a long waterproof, and a cloth cap covered his grey hair. 'Now, sir,' he said, unlocking the door, 'what part of the grounds do you wish to go to?'

'I want, if possible, to find the place from where that shot was fired,' answered Groom. 'That will be at some point almost directly opposite the window of the library.'

Payne opened the door and a gust of wind and rain swept in, almost tearing it out of his hand. Groom drew an electric torch from his pocket and switched it on. 'There's a short flight of steps, sir,' warned the butler as he led the way through the door, 'and they are rather narrow.'

Groom and Stephens made their way

down the steps, Bill flashing his torch to guide them while the butler secured the door. The wind seemed to tear at them with invisible clutching fingers, and howled in their ears as though laughing gleefully at having found fresh objects on which to wreak its fury. The rain lashed and stung their faces like a thousand tiny flails.

The butler joined them with difficulty on the squelching gravel path that ran at the foot of the steps, bordered on one side by a low privet hedge. 'Our best way, sir,' said Payne, raising his voice to make himself heard above the noise of the wind whistling in the bare trees, 'will be to make for the lawn.'

'Can you see the library window from there?' asked Groom.

'Yes, sir,' answered Payne. 'The lawn stretches right across the back of the house; all the back windows overlook it. This way, sir.'

Bill directed his light on the sodden ground ahead, and with their heads bowed to the rain he and Bluey proceeded to follow the butler along the path. Presently they came to an opening in the hedge, and Payne paused. 'There's a tripwire here, sir,' he warned. 'You'll have to step over it.'

Groom saw the thin wire glistening in the light from his torch. It was stretched at the height of about a foot above the ground and level with the edge of the lawn. They negotiated the obstacle and went on across the grass, their feet sinking deep into the soggy turf with every step. Once Bluey almost lost a shoe, for the saturated surface clung tenaciously. Near the middle of the lawn they came upon a second tripwire. The wind had dropped for a moment, and Groom took advantage of the lull to stop and survey the house.

The green-shaded lamp was plainly visible, although slightly blurred by the wet glass of the window. 'If we keep in a line with that light,' said Bill, 'we ought to come upon the place we're seeking. I should say it's about fifty yards further on.'

'How do you know that, Bill?' asked Bluey in astonishment.

'It's only a rough guess,' answered Groom, 'but I think I'm right. It's merely a question of angles. The bullet entered the window near the bottom sash and struck the opposite wall about two feet below the ceiling. An imaginary straight line, therefore, drawn between those two points and extended in this direction, would end somewhere fifty yards ahead and indicate the point from where the bullet was fired.'

'There's a patch of shrubbery about that distance away, sir,' put in the butler.

'Is there?' said Groom. 'Then I'm pretty certain that's the spot we're looking for.'

They continued on their way, and shortly reached the outskirts of the shrubbery Payne had referred to. 'You'd better be careful here, sir,' said the butler. 'There are two man-traps somewhere in these bushes, and I don't quite know where they are.'

The wind had risen again, and Groom waited until the squall had passed and shrieked itself to silence before he advanced. Cautiously parting the thickly growing, rain-soaked evergreens, he began to force his way carefully into the heart of the shrubbery. He kept his eyes fixed on the ground, flashing his torch this way and that, and saw the wicked teeth of a man-trap a yard to his right. He warned Stephens and the butler, who were following behind; but of the traces he was seeking there was no sign.

The shrubbery covered a slight mound, and towards the centre the bushes began to grow thinner and less close together. Here Groom suddenly came upon a small saucer-like depression. A little exclamation of triumph escaped him as he saw that the ground was trampled, and the branches of the bushes that grew round the edge of the hollow freshly broken in several places.

'Here we are, Bluey,' cried Groom, and the reporter forced his way to his side. 'This is the place from where the unknown murderer fired the shot that killed Miss Bingham. Look, there are distinct impressions of heavy boots.'

Stephens gazed eagerly at the churned-up mud. There were several footprints crossing and recrossing each other, and in the centre one pair that were deeper and more closely defined than the rest.

'That's where he stood while he took aim,' said Bill, with a note of satisfaction in his voice as he pointed them out to Bluey. 'Let's see if we can find anything that will give us a clue to his identity.' Heedless of the mud, he bent down and began to closely scrutinise the immediate neighbourhood. Not an inch of the ground escaped him, but he found nothing to reward his diligence.

It was Stephens who made the first discovery. The reporter was watching his friend at work, and happened to raise his eyes for a moment and look a little ahead. Something that glinted in the light of Groom's torch had attracted his attention, caught in the forked branches of a rhododendron bush.

'What is it, Bluey?' asked Groom, looking up sharply as the reporter passed him and picked out the object.

'It's an empty cartridge case,' answered Bluey excitedly. He handed the little brass cylinder to his friend, and Groom looked at it and slipped it into his pocket.

'That shows conclusively that the shot was fired from here,' said Groom. He continued his search, but presently straightened up and shook his head. 'There's nothing else of any importance, though we might as well see if we can follow the trail of these footprints. They should be clear enough in this soft ground, and will at least give us some idea of the direction from which the murderer came. What's on the other side of this shrubbery, Payne?'

'A gravel path, sir,' answered the butler. 'It encircles the lawn and joins the other path near the house.'

'And beyond that?'

'The rose garden, sir, which leads into a small orchard.'

'Are there any more traps or tripwires?' asked Groom.

'Several,' replied Payne. 'Particularly in the orchard, sir.'

'I don't think you need bother to come any further,' said Groom. 'I'm sure that we shall be able to avoid them on our own.'

'If you're certain it will be all right, sir . . . ' began the butler gratefully.

'Yes, yes, we can manage,' broke in Groom. 'You go back to the house and tell Mr. Vaizey that I will return as soon as I have completed my investigations.'

The butler made an attempt to bow — an attempt which nearly caused him to lose his balance, for a sudden gust of wind caught him unexpectedly at the same moment and made him clutch wildly at Stephens to keep on his feet. They watched him fighting his way across the lawn in the teeth of the wind, his long coat billowing like the sail of a boat until he was lost in the gloom.

'Come on, Bluey,' said Groom as he set off on the trail of the footprints. They were easy enough to follow, for a double line of them showed clear and distinct in the soft, wet mould, one coming and one going.

'He evidently went the same way as he came,' remarked Groom as they emerged from the shrubbery onto a wide gravel path. 'And to judge by the depth his boots have sunk into this gravel, I should say he was a fairly heavy man.'

They crossed the path and made their way over a strip of grass towards an arched opening in a high yew hedge. 'Be careful; here's another tripwire,' said Bill, as he sent a ray of light flashing towards the opening. 'By jove! It's been cut.' He looked thoughtfully at the severed ends. 'That's a rather interesting fact, Bluey.'

'How do you mean, Bill?' asked the reporter curiously.

'Well, it indicates,' answered Groom, 'that the unknown man must have been pretty familiar with the lay of the land.'

'You mean he'd been here before?' said Bluey.

'He must have been,' replied Groom. 'He would never have seen things like this in the dark unless he was looking for them.'

'I can't understand any man going to all this trouble to keep out burglars,' said Stephens. 'Besides, I thought man-traps were illegal.'

'They are,' answered Groom. 'And so far as the burglary explanation is concerned, I don't believe a word of it.

Vaizey is scared to death of something, of that I'm convinced — but it's not burglars.'

'What can it be, then?' asked Bluey in a puzzled voice.

'I wish I knew,' said Bill as they passed through the arch. 'I think it would go a long way towards solving the mystery. I'm afraid we shan't be able to find any tracks here, old man.'

The path they were traversing led under a rustic pergola twined about with the leafless stems of rambler rose-trees, and was covered with crazy pavement. The rain had washed the slabs of stone clean, and all trace of the footprints had disappeared.

'There's a chance that we may pick them up again at the other end,' said Groom, 'unless he branched off somewhere on the way.'

'Do you think Vaizey knows anything about the murder?' asked Bluey, returning to the point where the conversation had been broken off.

'I'm certain that he knows a great deal more about it than he admits,' answered

Bill Groom. 'He's keeping something back. I've never seen such a look of terror in a man's eyes before.'

'I suppose he couldn't have — ' began the reporter, and stopped.

'Committed the crime himself?' finished Groom. 'That's impossible, unless you are prepared to believe that Payne is also implicated, which I consider very doubtful. No, I don't think Vaizey murdered his secretary — but I'm convinced that he's a pretty shrewd idea who did.'

'Why on earth doesn't he tell us if he suspects anyone?' cried Bluey.

'That's part of the mystery,' answered Bill. 'But I believe one of the reasons is because he's afraid.'

'Afraid of what?' said the reporter.

'Afraid for his life, Bluey,' said Groom gravely. 'That's why he's taken all these precautions, surrounding the house with tripwires and man-traps and alarm bells. He wanted to keep somebody out, and he's found that all his efforts have been of no avail. The person, whoever it is, succeeded in killing Miss Bingham in spite of them, and that fact has filled Vaizey's soul with terror.'

'Do you think he's in any danger?' said the reporter after a moment's pause.

'I do,' replied Groom. 'I think he's in very great danger, and that it's remarkably lucky he's still alive!'

'I believe you've got a theory, Bill.'

'Perhaps I have,' answered Groom vaguely, 'but only time will show whether I'm right or not; and anyway, it's too early to discuss it at the moment. Of one thing, however, I'm certain, and that is that the whole solution of the problem can be found through Milton Vaizey.'

They had reached the end of the paved path while they had been talking, and come upon a second yew hedge similar to the other that separated the rose garden from the lawn. Groom's eyes caught sight of another cut wire. 'We're on the right track, Bluey,' he said, drawing his attention to it. 'Our man went this way.'

Beyond the hedge lay the orchard. Row upon row of fruit trees looked like an army of phantoms as the light from Groom's torch gleamed on the wet surface of their lime-washed trunks. The ground was composed of coarse grass that grew in tufts interspersed with patches of mud, and here the footprints were again plainly visible.

Winding in and out among the trees, Groom and his friend followed the trail. They passed two more man-traps almost hidden in the rank grass and, further on, still another tripwire. This had also been cut like the others.

The track led halfway across the orchard, and then suddenly veered sharply to the left and continued on until it reached a gap in a straggling hedge of hawthorn that appeared to divide the orchard from a narrow lane that ran on the other side. Nearest the lane, the hedge was reinforced by a fence consisting of four strands of barbed wire strung between wooden posts set at regular intervals.

On the lowest strand of wire, where it crossed the narrow gap, Groom found a clod of mud. 'He climbed over here,' he said. 'I think we'd better do the same, Bluey. Hello, what's this?'

He had been in the act of putting his words into execution when something on the topmost wire of the fence attracted his attention. He bent closer and, concentrating the light of his torch on it, saw a small dark object adhering to one of the bushes. Groom gently detached it from the spike and held it up between his thumb and forefinger.

Bluey leaned eagerly forward and saw that it was a narrow strip of soft leather — soaked in blood! 'What is it, Bill?' he asked excitedly.

'I think it's part of a glove,' answered Groom. 'The murderer was probably wearing gloves, and cut his hand on one of these bushes while he was climbing the fence. It must have been a pretty deep gash, too, for it appears to have bled a good deal.'

He handed his torch to his friend and, buttoning his overcoat, felt in his inner pocket for his wallet. Producing it and protecting it from the rain under the cover of his coat, he extracted one of the little seed envelopes which he always carried for the purpose of containing small articles. Into this he slipped the piece of leather and sealed it down carefully. 'It may form a useful clue later,' he said, replacing the wallet in his pocket.

Neither he nor Stephens dreamed at that moment that the blood-stained shred of leather contained an invisible clue that was eventually to lead them to the truth and discovery of Miss Bingham's murderer!

# 3

## Where Did Miss Bingham Go?

They managed to follow the footprints for a considerable distance along the lane, but presently it led out onto the Oxshott Road. Groom, realising that it was hopeless to try and track them any further, gave it up, and he and Bluey returned to The Priory by way of the high road and the drive.

Payne let them in and informed Groom that Inspector Browne had arrived and was in the library. A sergeant was standing in the hall and he stared at them as they divested themselves of their heavy coats, which by now were soaked through, and ascended the staircase. The door of the library was open and, as Groom entered, a man who was bending down examining the hole in the window looked round quickly. Bill guessed it was Inspector Browne, for he had 'police officer' stamped plainly all over him, from the soles of his regulation boots to the top of his bullet-shaped, close-cropped head.

'Who are you, sir?' he demanded in a loud voice that sounded as though he were speaking through a megaphone. 'I can't allow anyone in here while I'm conducting my investigations.'

'I'm Groom of Scotland Yard,' said Bill quietly. 'I've no wish to disturb you, Inspector, but I thought you might possibly care to learn the few facts I have discovered.'

'I should prefer to find things out for myself,' answered Browne brusquely. 'I learned from Mr. Vaizey that you had already examined the body, and must say that I was most annoyed.'

Groom regarded him steadily. He knew that many of the county police were jealous of the Yard and preferred to deal with any crime that happened in their district without invoking aid from London. Often the delay caused a murderer to escape, but the Yard was powerless to interfere until they were asked to do so. At the same time, Groom knew that many of the police were glad to take the advice of men more highly trained than themselves, but it was evidently not so in this case. Inspector Browne was very naturally anxious to extract whatever kudos there was to be had out of the conduct of the case for himself. Groom recognised the type of man, and instantly made up his mind how to deal with him.

'Then I understand, Inspector,' he said, 'that you would prefer me not to continue any enquiries in this case?'

'I should, sir,' replied the inspector shortly. 'I am perfectly competent to take charge and conduct the enquiry on my own.'

'You have no objection then,' Groom continued imperturbably, 'to my phoning the Yard and informing them that although I happen to be on the spot, you refuse to allow me to carry on any further investigations in connection with this affair?'

Inspector Browne hesitated at this and scratched the side of his large head. 'Perhaps, after all, we can work together,' he said gruffly after a short pause. 'I was naturally a trifle annoyed at finding that you had stepped in over my head, as it were.'

'I quite understand, Inspector,' said Groom genially, checking a smile at the sudden change in Browne's manner. 'Believe me, you shall have all the credit that is going. Leave me to find the murderer.'

'What have you discovered up to now?' asked Browne in a voice that was the pleasantest he could assume.

'Very little,' answered Bill, and he proceeded to relate the finding of the bullet in the wall and the empty cartridge shell in the shrubbery. He described the tracking of the footprints and how all traces of them had been lost on the Oxshott Road, but Stephens was surprised that he omitted any mention of the blood-stained shred of leather that they had found on the barbed-wire fence.

Inspector Browne listened attentively, nodding now and again profoundly, and when Groom had finished he carefully examined the misshapen bullet and the cartridge shell that Bill had handed over to him. 'It's a bad business — a very bad business,' he remarked, leaning against the table and pinching his fat chin between a podgy thumb and forefinger reflectively. 'I must admit that up to now I'm completely puzzled.'

'I'm at a loose end myself,' confessed Groom. 'I can recall few cases more extraordinary than this one. There's absolutely nothing to work on, for there appears to be no possible motive for the crime. Even the dead woman herself is surrounded in mystery, for beyond her name — and even that may be a false one — we know nothing about her. According to Vaizey, she had no living relatives and no friends. The only point at which we can begin our enquiries is to try and learn something of her past history that may provide us with the clue we're seeking.'

As Groom finished speaking there came a footfall in the passage, and Milton Vaizey appeared at the library door. 'Well,' he said, blinking rapidly, 'have you discovered anything fresh, Mr. Groom?'

His voice was a trifle thick, and Bill

guessed that it was due to the 'little restorative' he had partaken of in the dining room. 'No, Mr. Vaizey,' he replied. 'We're up against a blank wall. You say Miss Bingham was in your employ for eighteen months. Whom was she with before that?'

Vaizey shook his head. 'I don't know,' he said. 'I got her from an agency.'

'But surely,' said Groom incredulously, 'you must have taken up her references before engaging her.'

'She had never worked for anybody before,' replied Vaizey. 'I liked the look of her though, and as she passed all the tests I gave her, I engaged her. She was an excellent secretary.'

'During the time she was with you, did she ever receive any letters?' enquired Groom.

'No,' said Vaizey.

'Nor any visitors?'

'No. As I said before, I don't think she possessed any friends.'

Inspector Browne had produced a bulky notebook from his pocket and was jotting down the result of Groom's questions. Now he looked up. 'Was Miss Bingham in the habit of going out much, sir?' he asked.

'Very seldom,' answered Vaizey. 'She occasionally walked into Esher to do some shopping.' He paused. 'Now I come to think of it,' he went on, 'I believe that during one of these expeditions she made the acquaintance of a Mr. Robert Trevor, who lives somewhere round here.'

'I know him quite well,' said the inspector. 'So Miss Bingham was a friend of his, was she?'

'Hardly a friend,' said Vaizey. 'I don't know exactly how she came to be acquainted with him, but I remember her saying once that she had been round to his house to see a collection of native weapons and idols and things of that sort. She was interested in stuff like that.'

'Who is Robert Trevor?' asked Groom, turning to Inspector Browne.

'He's an explorer, sir,' answered the inspector. He lives at The Homestead, about half a mile from here. He bought it six months ago — just after his return from his last expedition in central Africa, I believe.'

'I think it would be a good idea if we went along and saw him, Inspector,' said Groom. 'He may be able to give us some further information concerning the dead woman.'

Inspector Browne looked a trifle dubious. 'It's rather late, don't you think, sir?' he objected.

'There's no time like the present,' replied Bill. 'In a case like this, delay may mean the difference between success and failure, and I'm sure Mr. Trevor will be the first to realise it when we explain what has happened.' He looked at his watch. 'It's just a quarter past twelve. It shouldn't take us more than a few minutes in my car.'

'All right then, sir,' said the inspector. 'I'll just go and tell Sergeant Paton to look after the ambulance when it arrives, and then I'll be ready to accompany you.' He put away the bulky notebook and crossed to the door.

When he had gone, Groom turned again to Vaizey. 'There's just one more

45

question I should like to ask, Mr. Vaizey,' he said. 'During the time Miss Bingham was in your employ, did she ever have any holidays at all?'

'She had two days off every month,' answered Vaizey.

'Where did she spend them?' asked Groom quickly. 'Here?'

'No, she used to leave in the morning and return late on the evening of the following day,' he replied. 'I haven't the least idea where she went.'

Groom's eyes lit up with a gleam of interest. 'But this is most important,' he exclaimed sharply. 'Why didn't you tell me this before?'

'I never thought of it until you recalled it to my mind, Mr. Groom,' confessed Vaizey nervously. 'The shock of this terrible business has upset me to such an extent that I can't think clearly.'

Groom looked at the man searchingly, trying to make up his mind whether he was speaking the truth, or whether he had been trying to withhold the information concerning the dead woman's periodic absences. There seemed to be no particular reason why he should, for he must have been fully aware that the fact was bound to come out sooner or later.

Groom, however, could not forget the look of fear he had seen in Vaiey's eyes — a look which still lingered there; and this caused him to regard the man's slightest action with a certain amount of suspicion. Not that he imagined for a moment that Vaizey himself was in any way responsible for the secretary's death, but because he was convinced that the owner of The Priory knew a great deal more about the strange affair than he wanted them to believe.

'Did Miss Bingham always make these excursions on the same date?' said Groom, continuing his questions.

'Invariably,' answered Vaizey. 'In fact, today is the first time she has missed since she has been here.'

'Today!' said Bill. 'Do you mean that today was the usual date for her to go?'

'Yes — the twenty-sixth of each month,' the stout man replied.

Groom shot a quick glance at Stephens. 'What is it that prevented her from going as usual?' he asked.

'I did,' answered Vaizey. 'I had a lot of important work for her to do that I particularly wanted finished by the morning, so I asked her if she would stay and do it. It only made a difference to her of one day. She demurred at first, but afterwards consented.'

Bluey, who was watching Groom, saw that although he was outwardly calm, Bill was inwardly labouring under the influence of intense excitement. To an ordinary onlooker the sight would have been unnoticeable, but so deep was the friendship between the two that every gesture and expression of his friend was unmistakeable, and he knew that in some inconceivable way Bill Groom had hit upon a clue. Bill's next words enlightened him — or so he thought — as to what it was.

'Then anyone who knew her habits,' he said, 'apart from yourself and the servants, would be under the impression that she was absent from the house tonight?'

Vaizey nodded, and Groom lapsed into

silence, staring thoughtfully at the carpet, his cheery face drawn into an unusual frown and the long fingers of his right hand caressing his chin. He was aroused from his reverie by the return of Inspector Browne.

'I'm ready now, sir, if you are,' Browne announced, bustling into the library. 'I've left full instructions with Sergeant Paton. Mr. Vaizey and he will remain on guard here until I return.'

A look that almost resembled relief passed across the fat, unhealthy face of the owner of The Priory. 'Will you be coming back, Mr. Groom?' he enquired as he accompanied Bill and Inspector Browne to the hall.

Groom shook his head. 'No, I don't think so,' he replied. 'We shall probably go straight back to London after our interview with Mr. Trevor.'

'Then I'll wish you good night,' said Vaizey, extending a flabby hand. 'I hope you'll let me know if you discover anything. I shall be most anxious.'

He waited while Groom and Stephens struggled into their wet overcoats, and watched them as they descended the steps to the waiting car. The rain had ceased; and the wind, although still blowing strongly, was nothing like as violent as it had been. A wan moon, struggling bravely through a feathery wrack of cloud, cast a pale, ghostly radiance over the house and the gaunt trees that surrounded it. Bluey, looking back as Bill Groom sent the car humming down the drive, thought that the desolate picture it presented was a fitting setting for the tragedy that had taken place there.

As they drove along, Groom briefly informed Inspector Browne of the facts he had elicited concerning Miss Bingham's monthly excursions.

'Where can she have gone to?' said the inspector in a puzzled voice when Bill had finished. 'It couldn't have been to see her relations, because it seems she hadn't got any.'

'So far as we know,' Groom corrected. 'As a matter of fact, Inspector, we know nothing at all about her at the moment. We've certainly got a little more to go on than we had, but it isn't much. I'm hoping we may learn some more from Trevor.'

They swung out of the drive into the main road, and Groom, following the inspector's directions, turned to the right. 'Of course,' he continued, 'it may be possible to discover where Miss Bingham went by enquiring at the railway station. If she was in the habit of travelling by train to her unknown destination, the booking clerk is almost sure to remember her.'

'I'll make enquiries first thing in the morning,' said the inspector.

His manner towards Groom had undergone a complete change, and he had lost the brusque, disagreeable tone that he had adopted at first. As Bluey remarked later: 'Browne was quite a nice chap when you knew him, but he wanted a lot of knowing.' This was entirely due to Bill Groom's personality, for there were few people who could withstand his charming manner when he chose to exert himself.

'Here we are,' said Browne, pointing to a white gate set in a carefully trimmed box hedge a few yards ahead. 'That's Mr. Trevor's house.'

Groom parked the car on the side of the road, almost opposite the gate the inspector had indicated. The Homestead was a long, low, rambling cottage built on the lines of a bungalow. It stood but a short distance from the road, and was backed by tall trees that grew so thickly that they gave the impression of a small wood.

A light burned in the window to the left of the little porch, and Groom turned to the inspector. 'It looks as if he's still up,' he remarked, nodding in the direction of the light. 'I'm leaving you to watch the car,' he added, to the reporter's disgust. Then, together with Browne, he passed through the gate and walked up the narrow path to the front door.

In answer to their knock, a sleepy-eyed manservant opened the door. He seemed astonished that anyone should have called at that hour and demanded their business. Inspector Browne gave his name and requested a few moments' conversation with his master. The servant departed, and they heard the mumble of voices. In a few seconds the man returned.

'Mr. Trevor will see you, sir,' he announced. 'Will you come this way?' He stood aside to allow them to enter the hall and, closing the door, led the way across to another on the left.

They entered a fairly large low-ceilinged room resembling something of a mixture between a second-hand book-shop and a museum. Strange native weapons covered the walls and strayed about in odd corners; and on tables and the tops of bookcases stood hideous idols carved from all sorts and conditions of substances. In the centre of the mantel-piece, amid an untidy collection of pipes and photographs, was a grinning skull, black with age. A large table to one side of the apartment was littered with books and papers, some of which had over-flowed onto the floor. The whole place was in a state of the utmost disorder, but in spite of this — or perhaps because of it — it somehow conveyed to the beholders an atmosphere of cosiness and comfort.

A man rose from a low chair near the fire to greet them as they entered. He was tall, lean, and bronzed from long exposure to a tropical sun; and his close-cropped hair was snow-white, as also was the moustache that shadowed but failed to conceal his thin-lipped, virile mouth. Groom judged his age to be somewhere on the wrong side of sixty, though his eyes, as he looked steadily at them, still held in their depths the sparkle and fire which is often missing in men of half his years.

'What can I have the pleasure of doing for you gentlemen?' he enquired in a deep, pleasant voice, looking from one to the other.

'I am exceedingly sorry to trouble you at this hour,' began Inspector Browne, 'but a terrible tragedy occurred earlier this evening at Mr. Milton Vaizey's house, The Priory, and we thought that possibly you might be able to supply us with a little information.'

'I shall be only too pleased to do anything I can to help you,' answered Trevor courteously. 'Won't you sit down?'

He dragged forward two chairs and, when Groom and the inspector were seated, continued: 'Now, please tell me, what has happened to Mr. Vaizey?'

'Nothing has happened to Mr. Vaizey,' said Groom. 'But Miss Bingham, his secretary, has been murdered!'

'What!' The old man almost shouted the word and staggered back, clutching the mantelpiece for support. 'Good God! You don't mean it! It can't be true!'

'It's perfectly true, sir,' said the inspector. 'She was shot from — '

'Look out!' cried Groom suddenly, and sprang forward just in time to catch Robert Trevor as he collapsed, a limp heap, into his arms!

# 4

## Groom Makes a Few Enquiries

Bill Groom carried the thin body of the old explorer over to a chair and tore open his collar. 'It's all right, Browne,' he said after a brief examination. 'I don't think it's anything serious. He's fainted, that's all. You might ring the bell for the servant.'

The startled inspector obeyed, and in answer to the summons the man who had let them in entered the room. He uttered an exclamation of alarm as he caught sight of his master, and hurried over to Groom's side. 'What has happened, sir?' he asked anxiously.

'Your master has fainted,' said Bill, chafing Trevor's hands and wrists. 'Can you get me some water — and some brandy, if there's any in the house?' he added.

The man nodded and hurried away.

There was a faint bluish tinge about the unconscious man's lips that Groom didn't like.

'I wonder what sent him off like that?' said Browne. 'You wouldn't think he was the fainting sort, to look at him.'

'Shock,' answered Groom briefly. 'I should say there was something the matter with his heart.'

The old man was beginning to show signs of recovery. There was a slight fluttering of his eyelids, and his hands twitched once or twice convulsively.

The manservant returned with a glass of water and a bottle. He set the bottle down on the table and handed the glass to Groom.

'Is your master subject to these attacks?' asked Bill as he sprinkled Trevor's forehead with the cold water.

'Yes, sir,' answered the man. 'He's had one or two lately. Dr. Compton, who is attending him, says it's his heart.'

Groom nodded. It confirmed his own opinion. He poured the remains of the water into a copper bowl that stood on the hearth and, opening the bottle of brandy, splashed a small quantity of its contents into the glass, then forced a few drops of the potent spirit between the old man's tightly clenched teeth.

It took effect almost immediately, for in seconds Robert Trevor gave a little shuddering sigh and opened his eyes. He looked vacantly about him for a moment, and then, as full consciousness returned, struggled into a sitting position. 'What — what happened?' he asked in a dazed voice, passing a shaky hand over his forehead.

'It's all right, Mr. Trevor,' said Bill soothingly. 'I'm afraid something I said caused you rather a shock, and you fainted. Do you feel better now?'

Trevor slowly nodded his head. 'Yes,' he murmured. 'I remember. You were telling me about — about Miss Bingham.' His voice sunk to such a low tone that it was scarcely audible.

'I'm sorry that I broke the news so abruptly, said Groom gently, 'but I had no idea it would affect you in the way it did. Perhaps under the circumstances it would be as well if we postponed our enquiries until tomorrow.'

'No, no,' said Trevor quickly. 'I should prefer to hear all about it now — at once. I am quite recovered. It was stupid of me, but I have not been well for some time. During my various trips to central Africa, I contracted relapsing fever — or, as it is sometimes called, famine fever — and I'm afraid that it has left my heart in rather a bad state.' His face was drawn and haggard, and his voice sounded hoarse, as though all the moisture in his throat had suddenly dried up. He stretched out a trembling hand and, taking the glass from Groom, drained the remainder of the brandy. 'You say that — that Mr. Vaizey's secretary, Miss Bingham, has been killed,' he continued after a slight pause. 'How did — how did it happen?' He forced each syllable out with an obvious effort.

Groom related briefly what had occurred at The Priory. 'We understood from Mr. Vaizey,' he concluded, 'that you were a friend of the dead woman's, and thought that possibly you would be able to give us some information concerning her.'

'I'm afraid, Superintendent,' replied Trevor, for Groom had revealed his identity, 'that I can't help you very much, if at all. I can hardly call myself more than an acquaintance of — of Miss Bingham's.' He hesitated slightly over the name. 'I only met her about three times.'

'How did you come to know her?' interjected Inspector Browne, and the bulky notebook appeared again.

'I met her in the post office at Esher,' answered the old man. 'She had been shopping and was rather laden with parcels. She dropped several on leaving the building, and I picked them up for her. I had seen her once or twice before, and as she was going in the same direction as myself, I offered to carry some of her parcels for her. On the way, our conversation turned to Africa; and since she seemed interested in the subject, I suggested that perhaps she would care to call in sometime and see my collection of curios. She appeared delighted, and said she would come on the following afternoon. She visited me twice after that. She was a very well-read woman, and most interesting to talk to.'

'Did she ever mention anything concerning her past life?' asked Groom. 'Anything that might enable us to solve the mystery surrounding her death?'

Robert Trevor shook his head. 'She never spoke about herself at all,' he answered.

'I understand that she was in the habit of making occasional journeys on the twenty-sixth of each month,' said the inspector. 'Have you any idea where she went?'

'No,' said Trevor. 'As I said before, I'm afraid I can tell you very little concerning her. She was the merest acquaintance.'

'Do you know Milton Vaizey?' enquired Groom.

'I've heard of him, of course,' replied Trevor, 'but I've never met him.'

Bill Groom rose to his feet. 'I'm sorry to have troubled you, Mr. Trevor,' he said, 'but I hoped you would be able to help us.'

'I only wish I could,' declared the old

man. 'It's terrible — terrible.' He tried to struggle to his feet, but Bill stopped him.

'Don't bother to get up,' he said. 'We can find our way out. Good night, Mr. Trevor.'

'You'll let me know if you discover anything?' said Trevor, holding out his hand. Groom assured him that he would, and a few seconds later they had left The Homestead and rejoined Stephens by the waiting car.

'Well, Bill,' said the reporter eagerly, 'you've been a long time. What happened? Did you learn anything fresh?'

'No, Bluey,' replied Bill as he took his place behind the wheel and started the engine. 'Trevor can tell us nothing more than we already know.' He gave him the gist of their interview with the old man as they drove towards Esher.

'It seems strange that he should have fainted when he heard about the murder,' remarked the reporter after his friend had finished.

'Oh, I don't know,' put in Inspector Browne. 'It must have been rather a shock for the old chap, and if his heart is weak — ' He broke off.

'Yes, I suppose that was it,' assented Bluey. 'But after all, if what he says is true, Miss Bingham was practically a stranger, wasn't she? What I mean is, the news seems to have upset him more than it should have done under the circumstances. What do you think, Bill?'

Groom apparently never heard him, for he took no notice and Bluey had to repeat his remark before getting any reply. 'I don't think anything at the moment,' said Groom without taking his eyes off the road ahead. 'There are several things that puzzle me, though; one thing being that if, as he says, Robert Trevor has never met Milton Vaizey, then why does he possess a photograph of the man on his writing table?'

'I never noticed that,' cried the inspector. 'Are you sure you saw one?'

'Yes,' answered Groom. 'It wasn't a recent one. It must have been taken some years ago, I should imagine. But there's no mistaking who it was.'

'I wonder how I came to miss it,' said Browne, a note of annoyance in his voice.

'It wasn't framed,' said Bill. 'It was lying loose on the blotting pad among some papers. You could scarcely have seen it, Inspector, unless you'd gone right over to the table. I saw it when I went to get the brandy.'

'Then Trevor must have been lying when he said he didn't know Vaizey,' exclaimed the inspector. 'I'll go and see him first thing in the morning and tackle him with it.'

'No, no,' said Groom quickly. 'Don't do anything of the kind. It would be a foolish move to make. It's possible that it has nothing whatever to do with the affair of Miss Bingham's death at all. There may be quite a simple explanation for the photograph, and Trevor might have been speaking the truth when he said he had never met Vaizey. On the other hand, if he does know more than he's told us, he could easily find some excuse to account for the presence of the photograph, and it would be the greatest folly on our part at the present juncture to let him think that we in any way doubted his word.'

They were running through the quiet,

deserted streets of Esher, and Groom brought the car to a standstill outside the police station. Inspector Browne got down. 'Good night, Superintendent,' he said, shaking hands with him. 'I suppose I shall see you at the inquest?'

'Most certainly,' replied Groom. 'In the meanwhile, I intend to make a few enquiries on my own. If anything comes of them I will let you know at once; and should any fresh developments occur at his end, you might phone me.'

The inspector promised, and Groom, bidding him good night, set off towards London. Throughout the journey homewards he remained silent, driving mechanically, his mind concentrated on the strange problem that Fate had thrown in his way. He was greatly interested in the case, for it presented just the kinds of unusual features that appealed to him.

Who was responsible for Miss Bingham's death, and what was the motive behind the murder? Why was Milton Vaizey afraid, and had his fear any connection with the tragedy that had taken place at The Priory? Groom was convinced in his own mind that it had. Some dark and sinister mystery surrounded Vaizey. Could it be that he was afraid of the same person who had killed his secretary, and was this the reason for the precautions he had taken to guard the grounds of his house against the possibility of a surprise attack? If so, from whom did he expect the danger, and why?

Puzzle his brain as he might, Bill could find no answer to these questions. He hadn't sufficient data to work on as yet, he told himself; he must acquire more facts before venturing to start formulating theories without any solid foundation on which to base them. At the same time, a certain vague, elusive idea concerning the death of Miss Bingham would keep thrusting itself upon his thoughts; and if it didn't supply a solution to the whole problem, it was at least a probable, even possible explanation for part of it.

Bill Groom was still engaged in pondering over the affair when they arrived in London. Dropping Bluey Stephens at his lodgings, he asked him to do no more than write a formal report for the *Daily Messenger*, and to get permission from the news editor to cover the case.

Groom then turned the car in the direction of his own flat and, having seen it safely garaged, settled himself in a chair to think matters over before retiring to rest, knowing that in the mystery surrounding the murder of Elsa Bingham lay one of the most baffling puzzles that he had ever attempted to solve.

★ ★ ★

Groom awoke early. The morning, in contrast to the previous night's storm, was bright and clear. Immediately after breakfast he telephoned Scotland Yard. After a short conversation with the assistant commissioner he put on his hat and coat and, carefully selecting a cigar from the carved cedarwood box on the writing table, hailed a taxi and was driven swiftly City-wards.

He had made up his mind regarding the direction which his enquiries should take, and the taxi set him down at the entrance to a block of offices within a stone's throw of the stock exchange. Groom ascended in the lift to the third floor and paused outside a suite of rooms on the glass door of which were inscribed in block letters the names Lang, Wilson and Lang, and underneath in smaller type, Stockbrokers. A few seconds later he was being shown into the private office of Mr. Lang, the head of the firm, and was accorded a cordial greeting.

'Good morning, Mr. Groom,' said the broker, a spare grey-haired man, as he rose from his desk. 'This is an unexpected pleasure. Sit down. I suppose you've called to see us about those shares we bought for you the other day. They've already risen several points, as you're probably aware, and there is every indication that they will go still higher.'

'I'm very pleased to hear it,' replied Groom with a smile. 'But that's not the reason I've called.' He seated himself in the chair which Lang indicated, and looked across at him with a smile. 'I want you, if possible, Mr. Lang, to give me a little information.'

Mr. Lang regarded him over the top of his glasses. 'I'll do what I can,' he answered. 'What is it you want to know?'

'I believe you're acquainted with Milton Vaizey,' explained Groom. 'Can you give me any particulars concerning him?'

The broker pursed up his lips. 'I've met him several times in the course of business,' he replied. 'In fact, we handle a lot of shares for him. But I know very little about him. What sort of particulars do you require?'

'Anything about his past history,' said Bill. 'Who he is, where he comes from, and how he makes his money.'

'I believe he originally came from America,' said Lang. 'I first met him about two years ago, and I understood then that he had just arrived in England. But I know nothing about his past.' He hesitated. 'May I ask the object of your enquiries, Mr. Groom? I trust that there is nothing, er, wrong that he — '

'No, no,' Groom hastily assured him. 'I merely wish to know for private reasons. I'm rather interested in a case that concerns him closely. His secretary was

69

murdered last night under mysterious circumstances.' He related a brief account of the tragedy that had occurred at The Priory, and the broker listened interestedly.

'What a terrible thing!' he exclaimed when Bill had concluded. 'Surely you don't suspect Vaizey of — '

'I don't suspect anybody at the moment,' broke in Groom, 'and certainly I don't think Vaizey could have been responsible for the crime. But I should very much like to know something further about him.'

'I'm afraid I can't help you, Mr. Groom,' said Lang, shaking his head. 'Nor do I know anyone who could. Between you and me, Vaizey has always been something of a mystery in the City. He calls himself a financier, but he hasn't got an office, and I don't remember him ever being connected with the flotation of any companies. Of course his dealings on the stock exchange must have brought him a big profit, but even they have been desultory and irregular — more of a hobby than a business.'

'And you can tell me nothing about him?' added Bill Groom disappointedly.

'I can't,' declared the broker. 'He must be exceedingly rich, for no one who was not exceptionally well-off could afford to take the tremendous risks that Vaizey has. The man's a born gambler; but where he got his money from in the beginning I haven't the faintest idea.'

Groom remained chatting for a few moments, then took his departure. He spent the rest of the day in the City, going from place to place, and putting the same questions to every influential man that he knew or could think of. But none of them were able to supply him with any fresh information regarding Milton Vaizey. The man's past seemed to be shrouded in as deep a mystery as that of his dead secretary's, and Groom returned to his flat after a long and tiring day without having added anything to his meagre stock of facts.

But of one thing he was convinced, and that was that the key to the solution of the whole problem lay at The Priory. The shadowy suspicion as to the truth

concerning the motive for Miss Bingham's death that had entered his head on
the previous night had grown stronger the
more he considered it. If he were right,
then the next move in the game was a
close and continuous watch on Milton
Vaizey's movements. Bill believed that
that way he would eventually hit upon the
truth.

By the time he had reached his flat he
had decided on his plan of action. That
night, accompanied by Stephens, if he
was available, he would return to Esher
and take up a position near The Priory
from a point where they could keep
observation on the house and the
comings and goings of its owner.

'What on earth do you expect to find
out, old man?' asked Bluey when Groom
called him up and invited him to join him
in the vigil.

'I don't know, Bluey,' answered Bill thoughtfully. 'But something may happen.'

Something was to happen — something that was destined to make the
mystery surrounding The Priory deeper
still.

# 5

## The Woman with the Pistol

Darkness had fallen, and a pale moon was throwing a soft light over the countryside, when Bill and Bluey left the railway station at Esher and set off at a sharp pace along the high road towards Milton Vaizey's residence. A damp white mist hung low over the ground, and the air was chill and wet, although no actual rain was falling — or, from the look of the clear sky, was likely to for several hours. The clean, wholesome smell of the fresh earth was borne to their nostrils as they walked briskly along, and Groom sniffed at it appreciatively after the stuffy, smoke-laden atmosphere of the London streets.

In a little under half an hour they arrived within sight of the entrance to the drive leading to The Priory, and Groom paused. 'We'd better stop here, Bluey,' he said, 'and discuss our plan of campaign. It is necessary that we should keep an eye on both the front and the back entrances, and to do this we shall have to split up when we get to the house. You had better take up a position in the shrubbery facing the main entrance. I'll go round to the back and do the same. If anything should occur, warn me by giving the hoot of an owl, and I will immediately join you, or vice versa. We've got to go very carefully, for we mustn't risk being seen from the house. If Vaizey suspects that he's being watched, any hope of our learning anything will be spoiled. Also, there is a chance, if my theory is correct, that someone else may be lurking about in the grounds.'

'You mean the murderer of Miss Bingham?' enquired Bluey, a note of excitement in his voice.

Groom nodded. 'Yes. So keep a good lookout, and don't forget the tripwires and those infernal man-traps.'

They made their way cautiously through the big gate and proceeded up the dark drive, keeping in the shadows of the trees that bordered it on either side.

The moon filtering through the arch formed by the interlaced bracken above them cast a mosaic pattern on the gravel — a pattern of ever-changing shapes as the slight breeze gently swayed the treetops. Twice they encountered trip-wires and safely negotiated them.

'He's had them fixed since last night,' whispered Groom. 'They weren't here then; or if they were, we would have broken them when we passed in the car.'

They reached the place where the drive bent almost at right angles and, turning the corner, came in sight of the house. Several of the windows were lighted, and they moved forward with additional care. At the mass of bushes that faced the steps leading up to the front door, Bill stopped. 'Here you are, Bluey,' he said, placing his lips close to the reporter's ear. 'Don't forget — if you see Vaizey leave the house, give the owl signal.'

He glided away among the trees, leaving Stephens to take up his position in the shrubbery. At the edge of the path that circled the back of the house he hesitated for a moment. To get to the place he had mentally selected as the best spot from which to command a view of the back entrance, Groom had to cross a patch of gravel. Not a vestige of cover offered itself, and he would be plainly visible to anyone who might chance to be looking out from any of the back windows. He decided to risk it, and stepped swiftly across the intervening space into the shadow of the hedge beyond.

He had reached his objective; but whether he had been seen or not, it was impossible for him to be sure. From where he stood, the entire back of the house was visible, and Groom saw that the library window was in darkness. Evidently since the tragedy Vaizey had given up using the room.

Groom knew that the owner of The Priory was at home, for before leaving London he had taken the simple expedient of telephoning him on a trivial matter regarding the forthcoming inquest. Exactly what Bill Groom expected to be the result of his vigil, he could scarcely have explained even to himself. He had only the flimsiest of suspicions, but on more than one occasion during the course of his career he had found success by obeying a subtle instinct that was little less than pure intuition, and he was following it again in this case. He was convinced that Milton Vaizey was the hub round which the whole mystery revolved, but how or why he couldn't say. Certainly he was far from expecting what eventually did happen later that night.

An hour passed slowly. The night was very still, and a distant clock striking was clearly audible. Groom counted the chimes. It was ten. The white ground mist was getting thicker — a fact which caused him some uneasiness, for if it continued to grow denser it would blot out his view of the back entrance altogether.

Presently, however, as the night advanced a wind sprang up, and before its chill breath the mist gradually dispersed. In spite of the heavy overcoat he was wearing, Bill Groom began to feel the cold. The damp from the rain-soaked ground was slowly creeping up his legs and numbing his muscles. Eleven o'clock struck, and still all was quiet. There was no sight or sound of life from the house in front of him. He wondered if the inmates had yet gone to bed. Perhaps after all they were to have their vigil for nothing.

Another hour dragged by, and the time seemed to pass on leaden feet. It was a monotonous job, waiting and watching, especially with the prospect that it might in all probability end in vain. Groom shifted his position slightly; he was beginning to get cramped. He would wait until three o'clock, he decided, and if nothing happened by then he would give it up for that night at least.

Half-past twelve struck from the distant clock, and the faint sound had barely died away when, clear and distinct, came the weird hoot of an owl from the direction of the front of the house. It was Bluey's signal! Something was happening, after all!

Swiftly and noiselessly, Bill made his way round to the patch of shrubbery where the reporter had concealed himself. He found Stephens awaiting him, and one glance showed him that he was labouring under the influence of some intense excitement.

'What is it, Bluey?' whispered Groom as he reached the reporter's side.

'Vaizey left the house a few seconds ago,' he answered rapidly in the same low tone. 'He's gone down the drive.'

'You're sure it was Vaizey?' said Bill.

'Yes,' replied Bluey. 'The moon shone full on his face as he came down the step.'

'Come on then, old man,' said Groom, his voice vibrating with suppressed excitement. 'We shall have to hurry up or we may miss him.'

They set off towards the drive and presently made out the stout figure of Milton Vaizey walking swiftly a short distance ahead. He had almost reached the bend, and even as they caught sight of him he turned the corner and was lost to view, shut out by the closely growing branches of the big trees.

Bill drew Bluey to one of the narrow strips of grass that edged the gravel, and they hurried on. Their footsteps were deadened by the soft turf and made no sound. As they swung round the sharp curve, they picked up the figure of Vaizey again, still making his way down the drive towards the gate. There was something furtive in his movements that convinced Groom that whatever the man's reason for this midnight excursion, it was one he desired to keep secret. There was, too, an air of nervousness about him, for he kept repeatedly turning his head to the right and left, shooting darting glances into the gloom beyond the avenue of trees. Once he stopped and looked back, listening intently, and Groom dragged Stephens quickly behind a big elm tree, believing for the moment that Vaizey was aware of their presence. But after a short pause the man continued on his way. He reached the gate and, passing through, turned to the left.

'I wonder where he's going at this hour, Bill?' whispered Bluey as they, too, left the shadow of the drive and started to follow Vaizey down the Oxshott Road.

'I haven't the least idea,' murmured

Groom. 'I hope he doesn't look back here, for there's not the slightest cover where we could take refuge if he does.'

Bill Groom's fears were groundless, however, for having once left the drive, Vaizey's nervousness seemed to have departed and he strode forward at an increased pace. Having proceeded some two hundred yards down the road, he suddenly crossed to the opposite side and, squeezing through a gap in the hedge that ran along the edge of the road at this point, disappeared from view.

Groom and Stephens followed quickly, and found themselves on a narrow footpath that twisted and turned among the straggling trees that grew close up to the hedge. As they went further along the path, the trees began to get thicker and nearer together, and at last became so dense that the feeble rays of the moon failed to penetrate them. Groom could no longer see the figure of Milton Vaizey, but the muffled sound of his footsteps and the occasional sharp snapping of a twig showed that he was still somewhere in front. It was very dark here in the wood, and Groom increased his pace a little in order to draw closer to their quarry, for he was afraid that in the gloom they might lose track of him altogether. If Vaizey turned off from the path, they would be unaware of the fact and miss him.

Suddenly Bill stopped and listened intently. He could have sworn that he had heard the faint sound of a footfall from somewhere behind him.

'What's the matter?' whispered Bluey.

'I thought I heard someone at the back of us,' Groom rejoined. 'Did you hear anything?'

Bluey shook his head. Although Groom strained his ears, the sound was not repeated, and after a second or two they moved forward once more. They were by now deep in the heart of the wood, and the path they had been following had frayed out into patches of coarse grass and undergrowth. Vaizey must have gone a considerable distance during the time they had paused to listen, for now not a sound came from in front.

Groom was beginning to fear that they had lost him, when he heard a crackling sound ahead — the noise of someone forcing a way through the thickets and bracken. What followed happened so quickly and unexpectedly that it caused Bill Groom to stop dead in his stride and grip Bluey's arm with a force that bruised the reporter's flesh.

From somewhere in front came a sudden shrill scream, instantly followed by two shots fired in rapid succession!

Recovering himself quickly, Bill whipped an electric torch from his pocket and, sending the bright ray cutting a path through the darkness, darted forward, closely followed by Bluey, in the direction from which the shots had sounded. They raced blindly on, scrambling among the trees and undergrowth. Suddenly, breaking through a screen of thick bushes, they came upon a sight that caused them to pull up and stare in amazement!

In a small clearing in the wood, plainly revealed by the light of Groom's torch, lay the motionless body of Milton Vaizey, face downwards. And bending over him, a still-smoking revolver clutched in her hand, her face bearing an expression of the utmost horror, was the figure of a woman!

# 6

## The Letter

At the sound of Bill and Bluey's approach, the woman looked up sharply, and with a stifled cry dropped the weapon she had been holding and turned to run. But Groom was too quick for her. Before she had time to take more than three steps, he had reached her side and caught her gently by the arm.

'Let me go! Oh, let me go!' she cried, turning a white, frightened face up to him. Bill Groom caught his breath, for she was one of the most beautiful women he had ever seen; and, in spite of the strangeness of the situation, he felt a queer little thrill run through him as his fingers touched the softness of her arm.

'Did you fire those shots?' he asked sternly.

She shook her head nervously. 'No, no, I know nothing about it!' she exclaimed.

'Please let me go!'

'I cannot do that until you give me some explanation of your presence here,' said Groom. 'If you didn't fire the shots, how did you come by that revolver?' He pointed to the revolver she had thrown away on catching sight of them. Her only answer was a stifled sob.

Groom turned abruptly to Stephens. 'Hold her, Bluey,' he said slowly, 'while I see if Vaizey is dead or only wounded.'

The reporter stepped over and took Groom's place by her side, while Bill bent down over the still form on the ground. He turned it gently over on its back, and one glance was sufficient. Milton Vaizey was stone dead. The two bullets had hit him squarely between the eyes, and had evidently been fired at close range, for his face was black with powder marks. Straightening up, Groom picked up the revolver and examined the chambers. It was a Smith-Wesson, and two of the six cartridges had been fired. There was not the slightest doubt that it was the weapon that had killed Vaizey. It was nearly a new one and, although Bill scrutinised it carefully in the light from his torch, there was no mark of any kind to show to whom it belonged. He slipped the revolver into his pocket and turning, faced the trembling woman.

'I'm sorry,' he said, and felt annoyed with himself that the sight of her evident distress affected him so much. 'But I must ask you for an explanation. A serious crime has been committed, and everything points to you as being the person who committed it.'

'I tell you I know nothing about it,' she reiterated between her sobs.

'Then how came the revolver to be in your hand?' asked Groom, hoping that she would be able to give some reasonable explanation.

'I — I picked it up,' she murmured at last, huskily.

'You picked it up!' echoed Groom. 'Where?'

'Here,' she answered in such a low voice that it was almost inaudible. 'After the man had thrown it down. Oh, it was horrible — horrible!' She shuddered convulsively.

Groom looked at her pityingly. 'What man?' he enquired.

'The man who fired the — the shots,' she replied. 'He sprang out of the bushes suddenly.'

'What was he like?'

'I don't know. It was dark; I couldn't see,' she answered.

'Then how do you know it was a man?' Groom queried.

'I — I — ' The woman's voice faltered and broke, and she burst into a paroxysm of sobbing.

Bill Groom crossed quickly to her side and laid a hand gently on her heaving shoulders. 'Come, come!' he said gently. 'You mustn't cry. If you're speaking the truth, you have nothing whatever to fear.'

She raised a tear-stained face to his, and her lips moved, but no words came, and it was some time before she had sufficiently mastered her emotions to be able to speak. 'I have told you the truth,' she managed to gasp at last between the sobs that still shook her slight body. 'I know nothing about this horrible thing — nothing!'

'How came you to be passing through the wood at this hour?' asked Bill.

His question seemed to startle her, for she looked up quickly and then nervously to the right and left. 'I can't tell you,' she murmured after a long pause.

'Do you live in this neighbourhood?' Groom was anxious to believe her story. His heart sank as he realised that this beautiful woman might be a murderess, so strong was the impression she had made on him.

The woman nodded; her lips were trembling so violently that she was incapable of speech.

'Where?'

She looked round towards the dark wood behind her and back again, but made no reply.

Bill Groom looked at her for a moment, then said, 'You are being very foolish in not answering my questions. Don't you realise that unless you can satisfy me that you are absolutely innocent of the crime, it will be my duty to hand you over to the police?'

She gave a little cry of terror. 'Oh, no,

no!' she cried, clutching his arm. 'Don't do that. I will tell you all I know; indeed I will!'

'I think you're very wise,' answered the young superintendent, 'for even if you are innocent, you are in a very unpleasant position; and if you're able to clear yourself of suspicion, the quicker you do it the better. What is your name?'

She hesitated for a second, and then in a low voice replied, 'Wells. Iris Wells.'

'Where do you live?'

'At The Beeches, my — my father's house.' Her voice trembled, and Groom thought she was going to break down again, but with an effort she recovered herself.

'Whereabouts is The Beeches?' he continued gently.

'Through the wood,' she replied, 'on the hillside.'

Groom thought for a moment before speaking again. 'Now suppose you tell me exactly what happened, Miss Wells,' he said at length. 'You can speak quite freely. My name's Groom — Bill Groom. I'm from Scotland Yard. If you can assure me that you have had no hand in the death of this man, I promise you that I will do all I can for you.'

The woman looked at him searchingly. There was sympathy in his eyes, and she realised that here was a man and not a machine, a man to rely on and trust.

'Bill Groom.' She repeated the name slowly in a low voice, and her fingers tightened their hold on his arm. 'I swear to you that I am entirely innocent of this — this horrible thing. I was coming through the wood when I saw him approaching.' She glanced for a moment at the body, and then with a shudder turned away. 'I think he must have seen me at almost the same moment, for he turned aside as if to avoid me. As he did so, a figure sprang out of the bushes and fired twice, and then turning ran away, dropping the revolver behind him. I ran forward and picked it up. It was at that moment that you appeared on the scene. I was horrified and tried to run away. That's all I know, Mr. Groom,' she concluded.

Bill regarded her steadily. Was she

telling the truth, or was she lying? He found it difficult to believe that she could have been responsible for the murder of Vaizey. But the fact that she had attracted him strangely must not be allowed to prejudice him in her favour. With his own eyes he had seen her bending over the body with the revolver still smoking in her hand, and certainly he had neither seen nor heard anyone else near the vicinity of the crime. True, she had explained how the revolver came to be in her possession, but the explanation was a very lame one — and yet in his heart Bill believed that she was speaking the truth.

'How was it you were able to see anyone approaching you in the dark?' he asked.

'I didn't until he reached the clearing,' she answered. 'The moon makes it fairly light here.'

'And yet you said a short time ago that it was too dark for you to see the man who sprang from the bushes,' said Bill, his suspicions returning.

'So it was,' she replied. 'It was too dark to recognise anybody, but it was just light enough to enable me to see that someone was approaching.'

'Did you know the dead man?' asked Bill.

The woman hesitated, and then nodded slowly. 'It's Mr. Vaizey, isn't it?' she said.

'So you do know him?'

Stephens saw her shiver. 'I've seen him several times,' she replied. 'But I've never met him.'

'Miss Wells,' said Bill suddenly, 'what brought you to this wood so late at night? Did you come to meet Milton Vaizey?' He hoped as he asked the question that her reply would be in the negative.

Her eyes opened wide with amazement. 'To meet Mr. Vaizey?' she repeated. 'No, of course not.'

'Then what were you doing here?' insisted Groom.

She looked confused and hesitated for a long time before she replied. 'I — I — came — for a walk.'

Bill Groom's eyes narrowed. 'Miss Wells,' he said, shaking his head gravely, 'you would hardly come out for a walk at this hour, and certainly not choose a lonely spot like this even if you did.'

'That's all I can tell you,' she murmured almost below her breath as she gazed at the ground.

'Which is as good as admitting that it's not the truth,' retorted Bill bitterly. 'Come, what was your real reason for being here?'

She raised her head, and her eyes held a look of pleading in their depths. 'I can't tell you any more, Mr. Groom,' she said almost desperately. 'I can only assure you again that I know nothing about this dreadful crime.'

Bill shrugged his shoulders. What was she keeping back? Was the whole of her story a tissue of lies? And could hers, after all, be the hand that had killed Vaizey? He shivered at the thought. On the face of it, it seemed likely, and on the evidence any jury would have unhesitatingly found her guilty. But Groom was doubtful. If she was clever enough to think out a story to account for the revolver being in her hand, she could also have thought of a feasible excuse for being in the wood.

Then, apart from that, there was the murder of Miss Bingham, and the precautions that Vaizey had taken to guard his own safety. It was almost impossible to believe that he had been in fear of a slip of a girl like Iris Wells. The whole affair was more puzzling than ever, thought Bill irritably. Just when he had believed that he was on the verge of learning something that would provide him with a clue to the solution of the mystery, it had merely become darker than ever.

He roused himself from his thoughts and turned to Bluey. 'We'd better let them know at the house about this,' he said, 'and also acquaint the police.'

'Can I go now?' asked Iris eagerly.

Groom pursed his lips and frowned. 'I'm afraid you can't,' he answered. 'You will have to wait until the police have seen the body. You were found where the murder was committed, and they'll want to question you.'

'What — more questions?' she asked in dismay.

'Yes. It can't be avoided,' replied Bill.

'You had better come to The Priory with me.' He turned to his friend. 'Bluey, will you stay here and guard the body until the police arrive? I'll telephone Inspector Browne from the house.'

'Aren't you going to search the body before you go, Bill?' suggested the reporter.

Bill felt himself go red in the darkness. His mind had been so full of the woman that he had forgotten for the first time in his life the ordinary routine of his profession. He walked over to the motionless figure and dropped on one knee beside it. By the light of his torch he began methodically to turn out the pockets one by one. There was nothing in the trousers but a bunch of keys, some loose change, and in the hip pocket a fully loaded automatic. Groom nodded to himself as he brought the latter to light. As well as protecting The Priory from a possible intruder, Vaizey had evidently gone about armed.

He replaced the things in the trouser pockets and turned his attention to the rest of the clothing. There was nothing at all in the man's overcoat. His waistcoat yielded a gold watch and a matchbox of the same precious metal. It was not until Groom came to the inside breast pocket of his jacket that he found anything of importance, and then his groping fingers came in contact with an envelope.

He drew it out and examined it. It was a cheap envelope, such as can be purchased at any stationer's, and bore neither name nor address. Groom raised the flap, which was unsealed, and took out the single sheet of paper it contained. As he read the scrawled lines of writing on it, he gave a sharp exclamation and started to his feet.

'What is it, Bill?' cried Bluey eagerly.

'Look!' said Bill Groom, his eyes gleaming, and held the letter out for Stephens to read, tilting his torch so that its light fell upon the white sheet.

It began abruptly without date or address, and ran as follows:

'You have failed to keep your promise. I warned you three times. This is the last. If you do not fulfil my

demands, you must bear the conse-
quences.

THE GHOST'

Stephens gave vent to a cry of
excitement as he saw the signature. 'Great
Scott, Bill,' he exclaimed, 'The Ghost!
Can he have murdered Vaizey?'

'It certainly looks like it,' answered Bill,
staring thoughtfully into the dark shadows of the wood. They both knew The
Ghost — an elusive personality that had
baffled Scotland Yard for many months. If
he was at the bottom of the mystery
surrounding the death of Milton Vaizey
and his secretary, Bill knew that it would
take all his skill and resources to solve the
problem and bring him to justice!

# 7

## Who Shot Milton Vaizey?

It was in a very puzzled frame of mind that Bill walked back towards The Priory, accompanied by Iris. The discovery of the letter had given an entirely new aspect to the case, and he was trying to fit this fresh development into its proper place among the other pieces of the puzzle.

'The Ghost' was an alias that concealed the identity of a mysterious and unscrupulous blackmailer whose exploits for the past year had worried Scotland Yard considerably. He had obtained enormous sums from various people, mostly those whose business or profession brought them prominently before the public, and to whom the slightest breath of scandal would have meant disaster and ruin.

His method was a simple one. He would seek out servants who nursed a real or fancied grudge against their master or mistress, and having found the type he sought, make them an offer of a large sum for any information, letters or documents concerning the private lives of their employers that were at all discreditable. The amount he paid varied in each case according to the value of the material supplied and the profit he thought it would yield to himself.

In this way he must have collected an amazing store of knowledge. Probably only in one instance out of every ten was the information thus gained of any use to him, for The Ghost never made a mistake, and was careful to select as his victims only those people whose bank balances were big enough to satisfy his extortionate demands, and against whom he held a secret of sufficient magnitude to ensure that they would be willing to pay almost any sum for his silence. So careful had he been in his choice that in not one single instance had any of the unfortunate people whom he had got into his clutches been sufficiently courageous to appeal to the authorities for assistance, and the police had only become aware of his activities by accident.

Several unaccountable suicides had taken place during the past year, and in three cases during a search of the private papers belonging to the deceased persons, there had come to light letters from this prince of blackmailers. But although the police had used every endeavour to discover his identity, they had failed to find out anything about him. No one apparently had ever seen him, and as far as this went his name was certainly appropriate, for he was a veritable ghost indeed — a phantom unseen and unknown, who spread despair and destruction in his path.

On two occasions the police had succeeded in tracing a butler and a lady's maid from whom The Ghost had obtained vital information relative to the past of their employers. In the second case it had driven the person concerned — a well-known society hostess — to taking her own life; but although both servants had been arrested and questioned, they could say nothing that was likely to lead to the apprehension of the man who had purchased the secret — which was in the form of old letters — from them.

They both told practically the same story. Each had received a letter from The Ghost making an appointment to meet him on different days and at different places. The butler had been instructed to be at an empty house at a certain hour. The Ghost had arrived punctually and the brief interview, during which he had suggested that the servant should try and find a document concerning his master's marriage — he was generally supposed to be a bachelor, and his engagement to the daughter of a peer had just been announced. The butler couldn't give even the faintest description of the man, except that he was muffled in a heavy coat and wore a mask. A further meeting was arranged at the same place a week later for the servant to report on his progress. During the intervening period, the butler succeeded in finding the document that The Ghost required, and at the second meeting the money was handed over and the transaction finished.

The case of the lady's maid was almost exactly the same, except that in this instance the interview took place in the deserted waiting room of a small railway station a few miles outside of London. This time The Ghost appeared without a mask, but his face was concealed in the folds of a silk muffler which he wore, and the maid swore that it would be impossible for her to recognise him again.

Try as they would, Scotland Yard could not unearth a single clue that was likely to lead them to the truth regarding The Ghost's identity. He was unreal, intangible — a name, and nothing more.

Was it this elusive criminal who had been responsible for the murder of Milton Vaizey and Miss Bingham?

Bill's keen brain was working busily, but in spite of himself his innermost thought was one of pity for the woman at his side. He was more than ever determined to find the murderer, for he felt certain of her innocence. Some intuition told him that whatever secrets she might have, there was no disgrace attached to herself. He knew that so long as he lived he would keep the memory of her sad, haunted eyes as he had first seen them in the wood, and hated himself for giving way to sentiment.

It seemed clear from the letter he'd found in the dead man's pocket that Milton Vaizey was in some way in the power of the mysterious blackmailer. He recalled a line of the text: 'I have warned you three times. This is the last.' Was The Ghost the person of whom Vaizey had been afraid, and was this the explanation of the tripwires and man-traps that surrounded The Priory? If so, how did Miss Bingham come into the affair, and what was the reason for her mysterious monthly journeys to an unknown destination?

The whole thing seemed a terrible jumble, without the faintest glimmer of a light to pierce the darkness of the mystery. Yet Groom believed that he was in possession of a single thread that might eventually enable him to unravel the whole tangled skein. His vague theory respecting the motive for the secretary's death had, to a certain extent, been strengthened by the murder of Milton Vaizey. But what *was* the motive behind that? As far as Scotland Yard were aware, The Ghost had never before been guilty of murder. But if he hadn't killed Vaizey, then who had? From the evidence of the letter, it was obvious that The Ghost had threatened the owner of The Priory more than once, for it distinctly stated that he had been warned three times before. It seemed feasible, therefore, to conclude that the blackmailer was the murderer.

Groom glanced at the woman beside him. If that were the case, how did she fit in? What connection had she with the strange sequence of events? He noticed how listlessly she walked, as though all her strength had departed, and almost unconsciously he patted the fingers that rested lightly on his arm.

Why had she been in the wood at all? he wondered. Had she been lying when she said it was not to meet Vaizey? If she had been speaking the truth, then what had been the object of Vaizey's midnight excursion? Was it possible that the dead man had gone out to meet The Ghost? It seemed likely, since he had the letter in his pocket; but that didn't explain the presence of Iris, or her reason for refusing any explanation when Bill had questioned her.

He suddenly discovered that he was thinking in circles, and that they all returned to Iris Wells. With an irritable shrug of his shoulders, he tried to dismiss the matter from his mind for the time being.

Bill had been so occupied with his thoughts that his sense of discretion had been purely mechanical, and it was with a feeling of surprise that he found they had reached the gate of The Priory so soon. He warned Iris about the two tripwires as they made their way up the drive, but he needn't have bothered, for when they came to the first one he saw that it had been neatly cut!

With a startled exclamation, Bill hurried forward to the second, only to discover that it had been severed the same way! They had both been intact when he and Bluey had followed Milton Vaizey less than an hour previously. Someone had visited The Priory in the meanwhile — someone who had been anxious that his presence should be unsuspected by the inmates of the house. Who could it be, and what was the object?

Groom hurried towards the house with a sudden feeling of inward excitement. The Priory was in darkness; not a glimmer showed at any of the windows as they ascended the steps to the front door. Groom, grasping the knocker, rapped loudly. There was no answer, and after waiting a few moments he knocked again. But still all was silent.

'I suppose they're all asleep,' said Bill, addressing Iris for the first time since they had left the wood. She nodded without speaking, and her eyes, had Bill been able to see them in the gloom, held an expression of fear in their depths.

Groom was in the act of applying the knocker for the third time when he heard the sound of a window being raised above the portico. 'What is it? Who's there?' cried the voice of Payne sleepily.

Bill walked down to the bottom of the

steps and looked up. 'It's me — Superintendent Groom,' he answered. 'Let me in, Payne. It's urgent. Something has happened to your master.'

The butler uttered an exclamation of alarm, withdrew his head, and closed the window. A few seconds later he appeared at the front door, an incongruous figure in an old overcoat which he had hastily assumed over his night attire. 'What's the matter, sir?' he began, and broke off in astonishment as he caught sight of Iris standing by Groom's side.

'Mr. Vaizey has been murdered — shot,' said Bill briefly as he took Iris's arm and entered the hall.

'Murdered!' The butler whispered the word fearfully. 'But he's gone to — '

'I've no time to explain now,' Groom interrupted. 'I want to telephone Inspector Browne; the instrument is in the library, is it not?'

Payne nodded in a dazed way.

'Come along, please,' said Bill, turning to Iris, and hurried up the stairs. He flung open the door of the room in which Miss Bingham had met her death, and then stepped back with a gasp of astonishment. Every light in the room was on, and the whole place had been thoroughly ransacked!

The drawers of the writing table were piled in a heap in the middle of the floor and were empty. The door of the safe gaped wide open, and in the fireplace was a great heap of burnt papers, still smouldering red in places, from which a thin spiral of grey smoke curled sluggishly up the chimney!

# 8

## The Cufflink

Groom rapidly recovered his habitual calm and entered the disordered room. A quick glance had shown him the method by which the unknown night intruder had gained access to the library. The lower sash of the window was wide open, and the top ends of a ladder could be seen projecting above the sill.

Bill crossed to the window. On the white stone of the ledge outside were several muddy smears, and these were again visible on the strip of polished floor that lay between the carpet and the skirting board. After a short scrutiny Bill came back to the centre of the room, and at the same moment the old butler, who had followed them up the stairs, appeared in the doorway.

Payne's eyes almost started from his head with amazement as he surveyed the untidy apartment. 'Good heavens, sir!' he gasped tremulously. 'How did this come about? Why, the place — '

'Someone has recently broken in,' said Groom, cutting short the old man's remarks. 'Didn't you hear anything?'

Payne shook his head slowly. 'No, sir,' he answered. 'Not a sound. Your knocking was the first thing that disturbed me.'

'Humph!' said Groom. 'Whoever it was could only have left ten minutes before I arrived. Otherwise those ashes wouldn't be still hot.'

He turned to the writing table and picked up the telephone. After some difficulty he managed to get a reply from the Esher exchange. Asking to be put through to the police station at once, he waited, tapping impatiently with his fingers on the table. Presently a sleepy voice came over the wire and enquired what it was he wanted.

'Is Inspector Browne there?' asked Groom.

The sleepy voice replied that the inspector was not on duty.

'Where does he live?' demanded Bill.

'Can you get in touch with him? This is Superintendent Groom of Scotland Yard speaking, and it's most important. Tell him that Mr. Vaizey has been murdered, and ask him to come to The Priory as soon as possible. Thank you.' He hung up the receiver.

Payne had advanced a few steps into the room. 'Is it — is it true about the master, sir?' he asked hoarsely, passing his tongue over his dry lips.

'I'm afraid it is, Payne,' answered Bill gravely. He glanced at Iris. She had sunk into one of the easy chairs by the fireplace and was sitting motionless, staring down at her hands that lay loosely clasped in her lap. So still was she that she might have been a waxen image save for the quick rise and fall of her chest.

'How did it happen, sir?' continued the butler after a slight pause.

'He was shot,' replied Groom, 'in the wood near here, close to the main road.'

Payne cleared his throat and drew a shaking hand across his forehead. 'I've thought something like this would happen for a long time,' he said in a low voice.

Bill Groom shot a quick glance at him. 'Why?' he asked sharply.

The old man hesitated. 'Well, sir,' he said, speaking slowly and jerkily, 'all these precautions he took to guard against burglars. The wires and the traps. And then he was so particular about all the doors and windows being bolted and barred at night. I never did believe that it was burglars he was afraid of.'

'What did you think it was?' enquired Bill.

'I don't know, sir,' answered Payne, shaking his head. 'Mr. Vaizey was nervous about something or other. He was always asking whether I'd heard anything in the night, or seen anyone hanging round the place, and he seemed as if he was expecting something to happen. And after the death of Miss Bingham, he got worse.'

'When did he first start getting nervous, as you call it?' asked Groom interestedly.

Payne thought for a moment. 'It must have been about three months ago,' he answered. 'That's when he first had the alarms and traps put down.'

113

'Have you ever seen anyone hanging about the grounds?' enquired Bill.

'No, sir,' replied Payne. 'I've never seen anything unusual at all.'

'And you don't know of any reason that would account for Mr. Vaizey's apparent fear?'

'No, sir,' said the butler again. 'But I'm certain that it wasn't what he said it was — burglars.'

'Have you any idea,' asked Groom, 'why he went out tonight, and where he could have been going?'

'Not the least, sir,' answered the old man. 'I didn't even know he'd gone out until you told me.'

'Was he in the habit of going out late at night?'

'I've never known him do such a thing before, sir,' Payne declared. 'Of course, he might have done. I shouldn't have known anything about it if he'd waited until after the household had gone to bed. But it seems strange, considering that he was always so scared of going out after dark.'

'Oh, he was scared of going out after dark, was he?' murmured Bill, his forehead wrinkled in a frown.

'Yes, sir,' replied the butler. 'He wouldn't even go out into the grounds after nightfall.'

Bill Groom lapsed into a short silence. Milton Vaizey had been afraid to venture out after dark, and yet he had taken that comparatively long journey to the place where he had met his death. Why? Whatever the reason, it must have been a sufficiently strong one to overcome his fear. Or was it that same fear that had driven him to take the last and fateful excursion? Was the letter the cause of the midnight walk, and had The Ghost possessed such a strong hold over him that he dared not disobey?

Groom could reach no definite conclusion regarding these questions. 'Do you think you could make some coffee?' he said at length, addressing Payne. 'I'm sure Miss Wells would like a cup, and so should I.'

The butler seemed startled and looked at the woman quickly as the young superintendent mentioned her name, but he made no remark beyond saying that he would attend to it, and left the room.

The coffee had been more of an excuse to get rid of the old man than anything else, although Groom was by no means averse to a cup of the hot beverage after his chill vigil. As soon as Payne had gone he walked over to the fireplace and, resting his elbow on the mantelpiece, looked down at Iris's bowed head. 'Miss Wells,' he said quietly, 'at any moment the police will be here. Before they arrive, won't you reconsider your decision and tell me the reason why you were in the wood at the time Vaizey was shot?'

She raised her head, and Bill saw that her face was deathly pale and drawn, while there were big dark circles round her large brown eyes. She looked thoroughly exhausted, both mentally and physically. 'I can tell you nothing more than I have already told you,' she said in a husky whisper.

'The police will not be satisfied; they will want to know more than that,' urged Bill.

She gave a weary gesture. 'I cannot help it,' she replied. 'I can say no more.'

'Won't you try and understand?' pleaded Bill earnestly. 'Don't you see that by refusing to speak, you are laying yourself open to the gravest suspicion? That you are, in fact, in danger of being charged with the murder of this man?'

'I know,' she breathed tremulously, 'but even that doesn't make any difference. I can't say more than I have done.'

Groom looked at her searchingly. 'Are you trying to shield somebody?' he asked quickly. 'Do you know who shot Vaizey, and is that why you refuse to speak?'

He heard her breath hiss as she drew it quickly inwards, and a wave of pity went through him. 'What — what makes you think that?' she whispered through lips that had become suddenly bloodless.

'What else can I think?' said Groom. 'If you are innocent of the crime yourself — and I believe you are — you can have but one object in keeping silent as to the truth of what you were doing in that wood, and that is to avert suspicion from somebody else who was also there — somebody you know: the murderer of Vaizey! For your own sake, please tell me.'

'No — no!' she gasped breathlessly, but her eyes dropped before his steady gaze, and she shifted uneasily in her chair.

Bill stifled a sigh of despair. He was certain that she was shielding someone. The tone of her voice lacked conviction, but he also saw that it was useless to question her further at the moment. She was on the verge of a breakdown, and a certain sense of chivalry forbade him from harassing her any more just then. He determined to return to the subject later, however, for he was convinced that his idea was correct.

Payne returned with the coffee, and Iris sipped the steaming fluid gratefully; it brought a faint tinge of colour to her pale face. Bill drained his cup and proceeded to continue his examination of the room.

The black japanned deed boxes had been emptied, as well as the drawers of the writing table. In fact, he soon discovered that there was not a single paper or document left in the room. They had all been destroyed.

He went over to the fireplace and, kneeling down, searched among the black mass of tinder which was heaped in the grate and overflowed onto the fender. But though he went through it carefully, he found nothing to interest him. The person who had burned Milton Vaizey's papers had made a good job of it, for not a single scrap had escaped the devouring flames. But what had been the object? Surely if it had been one particular document that the unknown intruder had been seeking, he would have left the rest and not gone in for this wholesale destruction.

Bill Groom left the fireplace and turned his attention to the safe. As far as he could see, it had not been forced in any way, for there was not the faintest mark or scratch on the door. If it had been opened by any other means than that of the key intended for the purpose, it must have been the work of a very skilled cracksman — a veritable king among burglars. He subjected the heavy door to the closest scrutiny, paying particular attention to the region of the lock. The result of his examination convinced him that it had not been tampered with. He straightened up with a puzzled frown.

It was obvious that the key had been the means by which the safe had been opened, and that seemed to indicate that it was Vaizey himself who had done so. Groom remembered having seen a safe-key on the bunch in the dead man's pocket. Could it have been Vaizey who had made such a holocaust of all the papers in the library? And if so, what was the reason? Had he anticipated that he was going to his death, and taken the precaution of destroying all personal documents that he didn't want to fall into anyone else's hands? It was certainly possible, but in that case who had been the person who had entered by means of the ladder and the window? Someone had certainly visited The Priory that night, after Vaizey had left, as the cut tripwires testified. Was this person the murderer, and had he come after the documents, only to find that they had already been burnt by Vaizey?

Bill bit his lip reflectively. Seldom had he met with a case in which there were so many unexplainable features. At every step he was confronted with a fresh complication that made the whole affair darker and even more mysterious than before.

He was standing near the open safe, his forehead wreathed in thought, when suddenly his eyes saw something that sparkled in the electric light. It lay at one side of the safe, about three feet away, and Groom stepped forward and picked it up. Holding it in the palm of his hand, he turned so that the light fell full upon it. It was half of a cufflink, and consisted of a square of black agate with a single tiny diamond in the centre. A portion of the gold chain that had connected it to the other part of the link was still attached.

Bill turned to Payne, who had remained, a silent and interested spectator, while he was making his investigations. 'Have you ever seen anything like this before?' he asked, crossing over to the old butler's side. 'Did Mr. Vaizey possess any cufflinks like this?'

Payne peered at Groom's outstretched hand, and slowly shook his head. 'No, sir,' he answered. 'I am sure he didn't.'

'What is it? Let me see!' It was Iris who spoke. Unnoticed by Bill, she had risen from her chair and was standing at the superintendent's elbow. He moved so that he no longer obstructed her view of the little object in his hand. She gave one glance at it, and with a stifled cry shrank back as though she had received a blow.

'What's the matter — ' began Bill, and broke off sharply.

The girl's face was ashen, and in her eyes was an expression of the utmost horror! She swayed unsteadily for a moment, and then, with a little moan, sank into Groom's arms in a dead faint!

# 9

## A Scream in the Night

For a moment Groom supported her, looking at the still-white face. Then, lifting her in his arms as though she were a baby, he carried her over to a settee and set to work trying to revive her.

It very soon became evident to him that she was suffering from no ordinary fainting fit, for every effort he made to bring her back to consciousness failed, and she lay like a log. He was seized with an insane desire to take her in his arms and kiss her — she looked so frail, so ill, so much in need of comfort — but he checked the impulse.

At the end of ten minutes there was no visible change in her appearance, and Groom, having tried every method he could think of to bring her round, straightened up and wiped the perspiration from his forehead. As he did so, there came a loud knocking from below. 'That will be Inspector Browne, I expect,' he said to the old butler, who was standing agitatedly watching his vain efforts to bring a sign of life back to the still figure of the woman.

Payne nodded and hurried away, and a moment later Bill heard the booming voice of the inspector proceeding from the hall, followed shortly after by the sound of his heavy footfall along the corridor. He entered the library accompanied by a small, dark man, and gazed in astonishment at the disordered room and the woman on the settee.

'Good heavens! What's all this, Mr. Groom?' he demanded. 'I got your message from the station and hurried along as fast as I could. This is Dr. Compton, whom I picked up on the way.' He introduced Groom to his companion. 'I understood that it was Vaizey who had been killed. Who is this?' He looked over towards the motionless form of the woman enquiringly.

Bill explained in a few words all that had occurred, and Browne pursed up his lips in a silent whistle. 'Miss Wells, eh?' he exclaimed when Bill was finished. 'I know her and her father. How does she come to be mixed up in this business?'

'I haven't the least idea,' Bill declared. 'She absolutely refuses to say what she was doing in the wood at the time Vaizey was shot.'

'Do you think that she can have shot him?' asked Browne.

'Personally, I don't,' answered Groom with emphasis, 'although as far as the evidence goes, including the fact that I found her bending over the body with the revolver in her hand, it would seem on the face of it as if she did.'

'Humph!' said the inspector, frowning heavily. 'It's a puzzling business, a very puzzling business. I wonder why she fainted at the sight of that cufflink?'

'I should say,' answered Bill, 'it was because she recognised it as belonging to someone she knows. I believe that her silence is due to the fact that she's trying to shield someone.'

'Your idea is that she knew the man who she says sprang out of the bushes and shot Vaizey?' queried Browne.

'Yes, and the sight of the cufflink confirmed her suspicions.'

'But how does The Ghost come into it?' objected the inspector. 'Surely she can't be shielding him? She wouldn't even know him.'

'She might not know him — as The Ghost,' said Bill Groom quickly. 'But don't forget, Browne, that his real identity is a mystery. None of us have the least idea who or what he really is; and if The Ghost is responsible for this crime, then it is understandable why Miss Wells may not have recognised him in his true capacity. I don't say that I'm correct, but it's possible.'

'You mean,' cried the inspector excitedly, 'that the real identity of The Ghost may be someone she knows very well.'

'Exactly,' answered Bill. 'Don't you agree with me?'

Inspector Browne looked thoughtful. 'It seems likely,' he admitted after a pause. 'Of course, you may be wrong in supposing that she's trying to shield anyone. She might have killed Vaizey herself, after all.'

'I think it's very doubtful,' said Groom, 'unless she's an excellent shot and can use a rifle.'

'A rifle!' echoed the inspector. 'But Vaizey was killed with a revolver!'

'Miss Bingham wasn't,' said Bill significantly, 'and I'm certain that the person who murdered Milton Vaizey was also responsible for the death of his secretary.'

'Yes, I suppose you're right,' assented Browne. 'But, so far as we know, Miss Wells may be able to handle a rifle.'

'Even then,' said Groom, 'she could never have made those footprints that Stephens and I followed from the shrubbery. They were made by a much heavier person. No, Browne, I think you're on the wrong track if you imagine that she's guilty. She knows something about it, but she never fired the shot. I believe her story to be true up to a certain point.'

'Well,' said the inspector, 'as soon as she has recovered we can question her about the cufflink. That may throw some light on the affair.'

'I'm afraid you will have to wait a considerable time, Inspector.' It was the doctor who spoke. During Groom's conversation with Browne he had been making a close examination of the still-unconscious woman, and now had left the side of the settee and approached them. 'Her condition is very serious,' he continued. 'She has received some violent shock that has temporarily affected her brain. Her father should be communicated with at once.'

'How long do you imagine it will be before she recovers?' Bill was unable to keep the anxious note from his voice.

'I am quite unable to say at present,' replied the doctor, shaking his head. 'It may be a few days; it may be several weeks. Her nervous system has been completely upset, and the only thing to bring her round will be perfect rest and quiet.'

'Then it will be impossible to question her for some time?' said Browne, frowning disappointedly.

'Absolutely,' declared Dr. Compton decisively. 'The slightest worry in her

present state might have a most danger-
ous and permanent effect on her reason.'

Groom bit his lip and turned aside.
Whatever might be the result of their
investigations, he realised that Iris Wells,
in spite of the short while he had known
her, already occupied a place in his life
that no one else ever could hold. 'Perhaps
her father may be able to give us some
information. You say you know him?' he
remarked, forcing himself to speak calmly.

The inspector nodded. 'Yes, very well,'
he answered. 'Colonel Wells is a justice of
the peace.'

'Has he lived in this neighbourhood
long?' asked Bill.

'For years, I believe,' replied Browne.
'Dr. Compton knows him better than I
do.'

'What sort of man is he?' said Groom,
turning to the doctor.

'A charming man,' he replied. 'A bit
brusque, but then all these old army men
are. He's been a soldier all his life. His
wife died about four years ago, and it
nearly broke him up, for they were
devoted to one another. He's never been

quite the same since.'

'Was he a friend of Vaizey's?' enquired Bill.

'No,' said Dr. Compton. 'I don't think they ever met. Vaizey had no friends round about here.'

Groom rubbed his chin with a long forefinger. 'What is the relationship between Colonel Wells and his daughter?' he asked at length.

'They are very much attached to each other,' answered the doctor. 'She worships him, and since her mother died I think Wells's whole life has been wrapped up in Iris.'

'Then they're not likely to have had many secrets from one another,' said Bill. 'I suppose Miss Wells isn't engaged?'

'Not as far as I know,' replied Compton, 'and I should have heard about it, I'm sure, if she were. I'm a frequent visitor at The Beeches. The colonel's very fond of chess, and I often drop in to give him a game.'

'I suppose I'd better phone to the station for an ambulance to take Miss Wells home,' put in Inspector Browne.

'Yes,' agreed the doctor. 'The sooner we get her comfortably settled the better. After you've finished, I'll get on to The Beeches and break the news to her father.'

Browne crossed over to the telephone and picked up the receiver. His conversation was brief, and while Dr. Compton was getting through to Colonel Wells the inspector made a short examination of the room, noting a few of his observations in his pocketbook.

Groom pointed out the fact that the safe had obviously been opened by means of the key, and Browne wrinkled his brows in perplexity. 'It's most extraordinary,' he said. 'I can't make head or tail of it. You say that the key was on the bunch in the dead man's pocket?'

'Yes,' replied Bill, 'I'm pretty sure it was. It was undoubtedly the key of a safe, and there isn't another safe in the house.'

'Perhaps it belonged to one at his office,' suggested the inspector.

'He never had an office,' answered Groom in an absent tone. His mind was busy thinking of Iris and her connection with the strange affair, and his answers to Inspector Browne's remarks were almost mechanical.

'Well, then,' said Browne, 'if the key was in his pocket, he must have opened the safe himself. Unless,' he added quickly as an idea struck him, 'he possessed a duplicate key.'

'That's possible,' agreed Groom, still in the same faraway voice. 'But how did the unknown intruder know where it was?'

'I don't know,' answered the inspector. 'It seems impossible to find any sense in any of it.'

Bill didn't answer at all this time. His eyes had narrowed to mere slits, and he was staring at the carpet deep in thought. An idea had suddenly sprung into his mind; a tiny speck of nebulous light as yet, but offering a possibility that, if correct, accounted for much that was at present inexplicable. It fitted in with his preconceived idea regarding Miss Bingham's murder, but he wanted time to elaborate upon it. At the moment it was so vague and intangible that he decided to say nothing about it to anyone, not even Bluey.

'There seems nothing more to be done here,' Inspector Browne's voice broke in upon the young superintendent's thoughts. 'Shall we go along to the scene of the crime, Mr. Groom?'

'We had better wait until the ambulance has been for Miss Wells,' answered Groom. 'My friend is guarding the body, and a few minutes more won't make any difference.'

Dr. Compton finished his conversation on the telephone, then turned to the others. 'Colonel Wells is coming over at once,' he announced. 'He is very upset to hear about his daughter.'

'Did he seem surprised that she was here?' asked Groom.

'Very,' said the doctor. 'He appears to have had no idea that she was out. He was under the impression that she was in bed.'

'How long will it take Colonel Wells to get here?' enquired Bill, glancing at Iris as she lay still and seemingly lifeless.

'Not more than five or six minutes,' replied Compton. 'He's driving over.'

'Supposing he were walking,' said Bill. 'How would he come?'

The doctor looked rather astonished at the question. 'He'd probably take a short cut through Boulter's Wood,' he answered. 'That's the most direct way from The Beeches.'

Groom turned to Inspector Browne. 'I take it,' he said, 'that Boulter's Wood is the place where Vaizey was murdered?'

The inspector nodded. 'That's right, Mr. Groom.'

'Does the path through the wood lead anywhere else except to The Beeches?' Groom continued.

'No,' answered Browne. 'The wood borders the grounds of Colonel Wells's place at the back. By jove!' he exclaimed as the object of Bill's questions suddenly dawned on him. 'You mean — '

'That it seems probable that Vaizey was on his way to The Beeches when he was killed,' finished Groom, a little gleam in his blue eyes.

'But why?' cried the inspector. 'He didn't know the Wellses.'

'Not so far as we are aware,' the young

superintendent replied. 'There must be some connection, however, between Iris Wells and the person who broke in here — otherwise why should the sight of the cufflink have affected her in the way that it did?'

'I give it up,' said Inspector Browne with a gesture of despair. 'It's too much of a — ' He broke off and turned a startled face towards the window.

From outside had come the sound of a shrill scream — a scream in which fear and pain were curiously intermingled. It rose to a high-pitched wail, and then suddenly died away into silence!

# 10

## The Man in the Trap

For the hundredth part of a second, Groom, Inspector Browne and the doctor gazed at each other without moving. It was Bill who first recovered from the paralysing effect of that terrible cry. In two strides he was at the door and went racing along the corridor towards the stairs, closely followed by Inspector Browne. In the hall they encountered Payne. The butler was white and trembling.

'What was it, sir?' he gasped hoarsely as they came up to him. 'What was it?'

'How should I know?' said Groom tersely. 'It came from somewhere in the grounds. Come and open the back door.' He hurried towards the alcove at the end of the hall.

With shaking fingers the old butler unfastened the door, and Groom and

Browne made their way down the narrow flight of steps onto the ground path. Here Bill paused for a second, listening intently, but all was quiet. 'The cry came from the direction of the lawn, I think,' he said. 'It wasn't very far away either.' He moved towards the opening in the privet hedge, the way he and Bluey had followed Payne on the night of Miss Bingham's murder.

The lawn lay bathed in the pale light of the moon, the gaunt, bare trees that surrounded it casting a tracery of shadow on the smooth grass. Bill Groom gazed about him, but he could see nothing to account for the scream. Then from the shrubbery at the other end of the plot of grass he heard a faint sound — a mixture of a whisper and a moan!

He set off at a run towards the patch of bushes and, forcing his way through them, presently located the place from which the noise came. It was a little way to the right of the saucer-like depression where on the previous night he had discovered the footprints of the unknown murderer and the empty cartridge shell.

On the ground among the bushes lay a dark figure doubled up as though in pain! As Groom approached, it raised its head, and Bill saw that it was a man — rough, unshaven and indescribably dirty. A groan burst from his lips as he looked up, and Groom discovered the cause instantly. One of the man's ankles was gripped in the wicked jaws of a man-trap!

'For God's sake, get me out of this,' he cried hoarsely as Bill bent over him. 'I think my bloomin' ankle's broke!'

With the assistance of Browne, Bill forced back the powerful springs of the trap and helped the man to his feet. He winced with pain as his injured foot touched the ground, and Groom had to support him under one arm before he could stand.

He was a disreputable specimen of humanity. His clothes were torn and plastered with mud, and several days' growth of beard covered his grimy, unprepossessing face. Altogether he had the appearance of a tramp.

'That's better,' he growled in a rough, uneducated voice. 'The man who planted those darned things about ought to be bloomin' well shot.'

Groom's lips relaxed into a grim little smile at the words. 'What are you doing here?' he demanded. 'Who are you?'

'I wasn't doin' anything wrong,' said the man in a surly tone.

'You were trespassing,' said Groom. 'You'd no right here at all. These are private grounds.'

'I wasn't doin' anything wrong,' the man repeated stubbornly.

'What were you lurking about for then?' asked the inspector.

The tramp remained silent.

'Come, you'd better give an account of yourself,' Browne continued. 'What's your name?'

'What's that got to do with you?' replied the man roughly. 'If I've been trespassin', isn't it enough that I've nearly had one of me bloomin' legs smashed in your — ' He burst into a flood of foul language.

'See here, my man,' snapped Groom, checking the torrent. 'You'd best keep a civil tongue in your head and answer our questions, otherwise you may find yourself in a serious position.'

The tramp was cowed at the tone of authority in Bill's voice. 'What d'yer mean?' he muttered hoarsely.

'The owner of this house was murdered not far from here a short while ago,' said Groom sharply, 'and the house itself has been broken into. So I advise you, for your own sake, to explain your presence here.'

The man started as though he had received a blow. 'Murdered!' He uttered the ominous word in a whisper. 'Good God! You don't think I had anything to do with it, do you? I don't know anything about it, I swear I don't!'

'I'm not saying you do,' said Bill. 'What I want to know is what you were doing in these grounds at this hour of the night.'

The tramp hesitated. 'I was only takin' a short cut to the high road,' he answered after a pause.

'That won't do,' said Groom sternly. 'No short cut would lead you in this direction. Come now, I want the truth.'

'Well, then, if you must know,' the man

sullenly replied, 'I came to try an' get a word with my wife!

'Your wife!' exclaimed Groom. 'What do you mean?'

'She works here,' answered the tramp.

'Who is she then?' demanded Browne. 'One of the servants?'

'I don't know whether she's one of the servants, or what she is,' was the reply. 'I only know that she works here — for a man called Vaizey. This is The Priory, isn't it?' In spite of the roughness of the tone there was a certain amount of culture in the man's voice.

'Yes,' said Bill Groom. 'What's your wife's name?' His pulse quickened slightly as he asked the question, for a suspicion of the truth had suddenly leapt to his brain.

'She called herself Bingham,' answered the tramp, and Inspector Browne stifled a cry of surprise.

'Good heavens!' he exclaimed. 'Do you mean that Mr. Vaizey's secretary was your wife?'

'Was?' said the tramp quickly. 'There's no was about it; she is!'

Groom shot a quick glance at the astounded inspector. 'You must prepare yourself for a shock,' he said quietly. 'She was shot last night!'

The tramp staggered back with a hoarse cry. 'Shot,' he repeated huskily. 'How did it happen? Who did it?'

Groom watched his face keenly. The man seemed genuinely surprised; and if he was putting it on, he was doing it remarkably well.

'We don't know yet who committed the crime,' he replied. 'That's what we're trying to find out. You say that the dead woman *called* herself Bingham. Wasn't that her real name?'

'It was her name before I married her,' said the tramp dully. 'Of course, her proper name was the same as mine.'

'What's that?' asked Bill.

'I suppose you might as well know,' answered the man. 'My name's Winter — Bert Winter.'

'I think you'd better come back to the house with me,' said Groom after a short pause. 'There are several questions I want to ask you. Can you walk?'

Bert Winter nodded, and with difficulty they proceeded to cross the lawn. Their progress was slow, for the man, in spite of his assurance, could only hobble painfully, and Groom had to support him at every step. The news of Miss Bingham's death — as Groom continued to call her in his own mind — appeared to have crushed him, and during the journey to the house he kept his eyes fixed on the ground. Once he opened his lips and Bill just managed to catch the one word, 'Shot!' muttered below his breath.

The old butler was still standing at the open back door as they came along the gravel path, and his eyes opened wide at the sight of Winter. But he made no remark, and Groom led the man past him into the dining room, where he sank into a chair with a gasp of relief. He was obviously in great pain, and before proceeding with his questions Bill called Dr. Compton and, briefly explaining what had happened, got him to examine the tramp's ankle. He had a nasty wound, but no bones were broken, and the doctor soon had it bound up.

'Now,' began Bill Groom when the job was finished, 'you'd better tell us the whole story, Winter. When you were married. The last time you saw your wife. And anything you can think of that is likely to supply a reason for her tragic death.'

Bert Winter gazed about nervously and cleared his throat. 'I don't know of any reason for her being shot,' he said, shaking his head. 'But I'll tell you all I can. I suppose you are detectives?' He looked enquiringly from Groom to the inspector. Browne had produced the inevitable black notebook and was waiting expectantly, pencil poised.

'Get ahead with your story,' said Groom. 'This is Inspector Browne, who is in charge of the case. I am Superintendent Groom.'

Winter's ferret eyes opened to their widest extent when Groom mentioned his name. 'Groom of Scotland Yard, eh? I've heard of you,' he said. 'Well, I'd better tell you the whole story from the beginning. I married Elsa Bingham five years ago. She was a governess then, working at Sir

Terence Gritton's place near Margate. She was always a bit above me in the matter of education, but I was well-dressed in those days and had a bit of money, and I suppose she took a fancy to me. Anyway, six months after I met her we was married at a registry office, and she gave up her job and we came to live in London. I had plenty of money, though she didn't know where I got it from.' Winter paused and moistened his dry lips with his tongue.

'Where *did* you get it from?' interposed Groom.

The man shifted heavily in his chair and dropped his eyes to the floor. 'I was a burglar,' he replied in a low voice. 'I might as well tell you the truth, because you'll find out, anyway. I told Elsa that I'd had the money left me and she believed me. For five months we was fairly happy, but then I began to go broke.' He hesitated and then went on. 'I'd had my eye for some time on a place that I thought was dead easy. It was a place near Hyde Park and belonged to an actress, and from what I'd found out there were diamonds there practically for the asking. Perhaps I thought it was *too* easy. Anyway, to cut a long story short, I had a shot at it and was copped. When Elsa discovered what had happened and learned that I was a crook, she wouldn't have anything more to do with me. I got a five-year stretch for the flat job. Elsa was in court when I got the sentence, and that was the last time that I ever set eyes on her.

'A friend of mine used to write me now and again though, at the prison, and he told me that Elsa had given up the house where we lived and taken a room in another neighbourhood. She'd gone back to the name of Bingham, too, so that there should be nothing to connect her with me. About eighteen months ago he wrote and said that she had got a situation with a man called Vaizey, and gave me the address.

'I was released yesterday before serving my full time, having earned remission marks for good conduct, and I came straight away to see if I could find Elsa. I hadn't got any money, except what they gave me at the prison before I left, and I thought perhaps she might help me. I didn't like to come to the house, so I hung about on the chance of getting a word with her, and got caught in that bloomin' trap.' He stopped and looked up at Groom. 'That's all,' he concluded.

A silence followed, broken only by the soft scratching of Inspector Browne's pencil as he finished his notes.

'Is there anyone you know who would be likely to have wished your wife harm?' asked Groom presently. 'Anyone who would have benefited by her death?'

Winter shook his head. 'No,' he replied.

'Did she ever speak to you about any relatives or friends?' Bill concluded.

'She was an orphan,' said the man. 'She hadn't any relations at all — not as far as I know,' he added.

'During the time she was in the employ of Mr. Vaizey,' said Groom, 'she used to have two days off every month which she spent away from The Priory. Have you any idea where she went, or whom she went to see?'

'Yes, I can tell you that,' said Winter,

and Inspector Browne raised his eyes sharply from his notebook at the man's reply. 'About six months after I was pinched I heard through my pal that she had given birth to a child. It was after this that she gave up the house and took a furnished room in her own name. She sent the baby to a home in Margate — she was friendly with the matron when she was working at Gretton's place — and on the twenty-sixth of every month she used to go and see the kid and pay the money due for its keep.'

'So that's the explanation for her periodic journeys,' murmured Groom almost to himself. 'I suppose you're sure of this?'

'Yes,' answered Bert Winter. 'My friend told me all about it in one of his letters. Before I was sent to prison I asked him to keep an eye on Elsa for me, and let me know what she was doing.'

Groom stared thoughtfully at the floor, his mobile lips compressed into a thin line. Although he had discovered the reason for the dead woman's monthly visits and where she had gone, it did little or nothing towards clearing up the tangle. Indeed, if anything, it only served to make it darker and more impenetrable than before, for apparently they had nothing whatever to do with the mystery that surrounded The Priory. The deaths of Milton Vaizey and his secretary were as puzzling as ever.

Inspector Browne shut his notebook with a snap and looked across at Winter. 'You know nothing about the murder?' he asked the man suspiciously. 'You're sure you had no hand in that?'

'Me!' cried the man. 'No, I didn't know anything about it until you told me.'

'How long had you been lurking about the grounds before you got caught in the trap?' said Groom.

'Not more'n ten or fifteen minutes,' answered Winter. 'It took me a fair time to find the place.'

'You didn't see anyone else hanging round the house?' asked Bill.

'I didn't see no one,' Winter replied.

'Did you get into the grounds by way of the drive?' continued Groom.

'No,' said the man, shaking his head. 'I

came up a sort of lane and through an orchard.'

Groom nodded. It was the same way he and Bluey had tracked the footprints of Miss Bingham — or rather Mrs. Winter's murderer. 'Have you ever heard of The Ghost?' He snapped out the question suddenly, watching to see what effect it had upon Winter.

The man's face depicted the utmost amazement. 'The ghost,' he repeated, staring at Bill as though he had taken leave of his senses. 'What ghost? Is the bloomin' place haunted?'

Groom's lips curved into a faint smile. 'No. The Ghost is a criminal,' he explained. 'A blackmailer of the worst kind.'

'I've never heard of him,' replied Winter. 'Why? Has it got anything to do with the murder of Elsa and this man Vaizey?'

'Quite a lot, I fancy,' said Bill shortly. He turned to Inspector Browne. 'I wish that ambulance would hurry up. Stephens will be wondering what has happened.'

'It ought to be here by now,' replied the

inspector, and as if in answer to his words there came the sound of a car drawing up outside, followed a second later by a loud knocking on the front door.

'That's it,' said Browne, and crossing to the door, he passed out into the hall.

He proved to be wrong as regards the ambulance, however, for presently Groom heard a deep voice exclaim: 'Is that you, Browne? Where's Compton? How's my daughter?'

There was a rumble of voices, and then the sound of heavy footfalls ascending the stairs. A few moments afterwards, Inspector Browne came back into the dining room. 'It was Colonel Wells,' he said unnecessarily. 'He's gone up to the library with Dr. Compton.'

'I should like a word with him,' said Bill. 'Will you stay with Winter?'

Browne nodded, and Groom left the dining room and made his way up the stairs. A tall, broad-shouldered man was bending over the settee talking to Dr. Compton as he entered. He looked up quickly as Bill approached.

'This is Colonel Wells,' said the doctor,

introducing Groom, and the two men shook hands.

There was no mistaking Colonel Wells's profession, for its characteristics were stamped indelibly all over him: his military carriage, close-cropped iron-grey hair and moustache, stubborn fighting jaw and sharp, decisive manner of speech all proclaimed the soldier. His face was lined and haggard, and there was a look of trouble in his rather pronounced steely blue eyes as they encountered Groom's gaze.

'It's a very distressing business,' he said, looking anxiously at the still form of his daughter. 'I understand that you were in the room when Iris fainted, Mr. Groom. Can you tell me anything to account for this sudden seizure?'

'I was hoping that *you* might be able to tell *us*,' said Groom quietly. 'It was this, apparently, that was the cause of the mischief.' He took the broken cufflink from his pocket and held it out.

The colonel regarded it curiously; and Groom, who was watching the man keenly, thought that his face went a shade paler. 'Have you ever seen anything like it before?' he asked.

Colonel Wells hesitated for a fraction of a second before he replied — a fact that Bill noted. 'No,' he said at length. 'I can't see how this could have been the cause of Iris's illness.'

'Well, it was,' replied Groom. 'There's not a doubt of it.'

'How did it come into your possession, Mr. Groom?' enquired the colonel.

'I found it while I was making an examination of this room,' answered Bill, his eyes fixed on Wells's face. 'It was undoubtedly dropped by the person who broke in.'

'It's a most amazing affair,' said the colonel. 'Is it true that Vaizey, the owner of the place, has been murdered?'

Groom nodded. 'Did you know him?' he asked.

'I never met the man in my life,' Wells declared. 'I was never more surprised than when Compton phoned and said Iris was at The Priory. How did she get here?'

Groom related all the details of the crime, and Wells listened with close attention. 'I can't understand it,' he exclaimed after Bill had finished. 'First his secretary, and now Vaizey himself. Have you any theory to account for it, Mr. Groom?'

'Several,' answered Groom evasively. 'But at the moment I haven't sufficient facts in my possession to warrant disclosing them. Can you offer any explanation for your daughter's presence in the wood at the time Vaizey was shot?'

'I can't,' replied the colonel. 'I was under the impression that she was in bed and asleep.'

'I suppose she couldn't have gone with the intention of meeting Vaizey?' said Groom.

'I don't know just what you are suggesting, Mr. Groom,' Wells began stiffly, 'but — '

'I'm not suggesting anything,' interrupted Groom. 'You must forgive me, Colonel Wells, if my question annoys you. But I am a detective, as you are aware, and am doing my utmost to find out the truth that lies at the bottom of this mystery. It's obvious that your daughter is in some way mixed up in it, and I should be neglecting my duty if I failed to try and discover how; you must realise that. I personally believe that your daughter is innocent, but the sooner the matter is cleared up the better it will be for her.'

The colonel's brow cleared, and he nodded. 'I'm sorry, Mr. Groom,' he said. 'I quite realise your position. But it's absolutely impossible that Iris could have had any reason for meeting Milton Vaizey. He was as much a stranger to her as he was to me.'

'She might have been acquainted with him without your knowledge,' Groom persisted.

'I'm sure she wasn't,' replied the colonel emphatically. 'If she had been, she would have told me. We have no secrets from each other.'

'Then what can she possibly have been doing at that place at such an hour?' asked Bill.

'She told you she was taking a walk.'

'No woman would choose to stroll in a dark wood at that time of night without some very pressing reason. Besides, it wouldn't account for her obvious agitation at my questions and her sudden collapse at the sight of that cufflink.'

Before Colonel Wells could reply, the ambulance arrived. Groom lifted Iris in his arms tenderly and, carrying her carefully downstairs, placed her comfortably in the vehicle. Sergeant Paton and a constable had come with it, and Inspector Browne ordered the sergeant to keep watch on Winter while he came out and instructed the driver of the ambulance to return to The Priory after he had conveyed Iris Wells to her home.

'Get her to bed as quickly as possible,' said the doctor to Colonel Wells as the latter took his place in the little two-seater car in which he had driven over. 'And give her plenty of hot-water bottles. I'll come along as soon as I've finished here.'

The ambulance drove off, followed by the colonel's car, and Bill stood gazing after it until Inspector Browne touched him on the arm. 'Now, Mr. Groom,' he said, 'I think we'd better go to Boulter's Wood without further delay.'

Bill agreed, and he and the inspector

set off, accompanied by the doctor and the constable.

They arrived to find Bluey just closing his notebook, in which he had evidently been writing a report for the *Messenger*. 'You have been a time, Bill,' he grunted. 'What kept you so long?' It had been a dreary and gruesome night for Bluey, waiting there in the clearing with only the dead body of Milton Vaizey for company, and not a sound breaking the hushed silence.

Groom explained the cause of his long absence, while the doctor made a short examination of the body and Inspector Browne and the constable searched in the vicinity for some possible clue.

'Do you think that this man Winter could have had anything to do with the murder?' asked the reporter thoughtfully, when he had heard the whole story.

'I should say it was very doubtful, old man,' answered Bill. 'What possible motive could he have?'

'That's true,' agreed Bluey. 'But he might have been the person who broke into the library.'

'And left behind the diamond-and-agate cufflink?' said Bill, shaking his head. 'No, I'm sure you're wrong there also, Bluey. I'm inclined to believe Winter's story. I think that he was merely hanging about, as he says, on the off chance of getting a word with his wife. Whoever it was who entered The Priory and destroyed those papers had been there before. All the tripwires in the drive were cut, don't forget that!'

'It's certainly a puzzle,' grunted Stephens. 'I've been thinking while I was waiting for you to come back, Bill, and I've got an idea. From the letter you found on Vaizey, it seems pretty clear that he was being blackmailed by The Ghost, doesn't it?'

'Go on,' said Bill interestedly, as his friend paused.

'In that case,' continued Bluey, 'at first sight it looks as if it rather lets The Ghost off so far as the murder is concerned. For if he had a hold on Vaizey, and was hoping to extract money from him, it's ridiculous to believe that he shot him. He wouldn't have any motive for the crime. It would be rather like killing the goose that was going to lay the golden eggs.'

'Yes, I see what you mean,' said Groom, 'but — '

'Wait a minute, Bill,' broke in the reporter. 'Supposing, however, that in some way Vaizey had discovered The Ghost's real identity. That would supply a motive, wouldn't it?'

'Certainly it would,' answered Groom. 'But you've forgotten Miss Bingham.'

'No, I haven't,' replied Bluey excitedly. 'I believe that Vaizey took her into his confidence. He probably knew that The Ghost was aware he had found out who he was, and told Miss Bingham in case anything should happen to him. We know that he was afraid of something. I think that The Ghost killed both Vaizey and his secretary, so that they shouldn't be able to disclose his identity.'

'It's not a bad theory, Bluey,' said Groom, 'but I don't think it's the right one.'

'Why, what's wrong with it?' demanded the reporter.

'Several things,' replied the superintendent. 'It doesn't account for Iris Wells's connection with the affair, for one; or why, if Vaizey was so afraid of The Ghost, he should have come here in the middle of the night, for another. The greatest thing against it, however, to my mind, is the fact that although I am sure it was the same hand that killed both Vaizey and Miss Bingham, I'm equally certain that in her case her death was due to pure accident!'

Stephens stared at his friend in blank astonishment. 'Accident? What do you mean?'

'Simply this,' replied Bill. 'That she was shot in mistake for Milton Vaizey.'

# 11

## At Scotland Yard

If Bill Groom had suddenly announced that he himself had been responsible for the woman's death, Bluey could not have looked more amazed. His jaw dropped, and for several seconds he was so astounded that he could only gaze at his friend in blank, petrified silence.

A faint smile curved the corners of Groom's mouth as he noted the effect that his quietly spoken words had upon the reporter.

'But I — I don't understand,' stammered Bluey at last, finding his voice. 'How on earth could she have been shot in mistake for Vaizey?'

'Quite easily, Bluey,' replied Bill in a low tone. He looked round to see if the others were within earshot before continuing, but Inspector Browne and the constable had moved further away and were searching about among the bushes that bordered the clearing. Dr. Compton was still engaged upon his examination of the body, and appeared to be engrossed in his task.

'The possibility of the idea struck me from the first,' Groom went on, after he had assured himself that he could not be overheard. 'The moment, in fact, that I saw that look of fear in Vaizey's eyes, and learned of the precautions he had taken to guard The Priory, it was obvious that the man was frightened for his own safety.'

'But how could the murderer have possibly made such a mistake?' said Bluey. 'Surely he would have recognised Miss Bingham while he was taking aim.'

Groom shook his head. 'Not necessarily,' he replied. 'Don't forget that she wore her hair Eton-cropped, and that she was dressed in a tailor-made costume, collar and tie. In the dim light from the green-shaded lamp, and seated with her back to the window, it would have been quite easy for anyone to have mistaken her for a man — and, since she was occupying the chair in which Vaizey usually sat, for Vaizey himself. Added to which, the glass of the window must have been so blurred by the rain that the murderer, from his position in the shrubbery, would have had only a very hazy view of her.'

'I see,' said Bluey, nodding. 'I'm beginning to believe you're right, old man.'

'I'm convinced that I am,' said Bill. 'Vaizey's death coming almost immediately after, and Bert Winter's story, have helped to confirm my theory. If it's correct, it explains a lot, whereas otherwise there is no motive that we know of to account for the woman being shot.'

'It only tends to strengthen my idea, Bill,' said Bluey. 'The Ghost wanted to get rid of Vaizey because he had found out his real identity. Then, discovering that he had made a mistake with Miss Bingham, he lured Vaizey here and killed him.'

'How did he lure him here?' asked Groom.

'Why, by means of the letter, of course!'

replied the reporter. 'Don't you see how it all fits in?'

'There's nothing in the letter suggesting a meeting,' disagreed his friend. 'It merely contains a warning and a veiled threat.'

'Yes, that's true,' admitted Stephens. 'But perhaps Vaizey had met The Ghost here before.'

Bill pursed his lips in dissent. 'If Vaizey had been so afraid of The Ghost that he surrounded his house with traps and alarms to keep him away,' he replied, 'no power on earth would ever have induced him to risk a meeting with the man. The law of self-preservation comes above everything, Bluey; and no matter to what extent The Ghost held him in his clutches, it wouldn't have been strong enough to have brought Vaizey out to what he must have known was almost certain death. Besides, how does Miss Wells come into it? You mustn't forget her. What was she doing in the wood, and why did the sight of that cufflink have such an effect on her that it produced a shock from which it is doubtful she will recover for several days?'

'There might have been some sort of an understanding between her and Vaizey,' suggested the reporter. 'Perhaps he didn't come to meet The Ghost, but to meet her.'

'The same idea crossed my own mind,' said Bill Groom, 'and I questioned Colonel Wells about it, but he says that his daughter didn't know Vaizey.'

'She might have done so without telling her father,' said Bluey.

'She doesn't strike me as being the sort of woman to carry on a clandestine intrigue,' replied Bill stiffly, 'particularly with a man of Vaizey's type. If he had been young and good-looking, it might be a different matter altogether, but as it is — ' He broke off. 'No, there's some other explanation, Bluey, I'm sure.'

'Well, anyway,' said Stephens, 'one thing's pretty certain, and that is that it was The Ghost who killed Milton Vaizey and his secretary.'

'I don't agree with you,' answered Groom. 'Personally I don't think The Ghost was responsible for either of the murders.'

'What!' cried Bluey. 'Then who *do* you think committed the crimes?'

'Not so loud!' admonished his friend. 'I don't know yet, but I have a rather strong suspicion. I'm waiting for some further facts to confirm it.'

Bluey waited, looking at Bill expectantly, hoping that he would continue. But his friend remained silent. 'Have you discovered anything fresh that you haven't told me about, Bill?' he asked after a pause.

'No,' said Groom. 'You know all that I know. I'm not going to say any more at the moment, Bluey. Try and think it out for yourself, and see if you can find a theory that will cover all the facts in our possession. See if you can find some connection between facts and events which seem at the moment unconnected. And when you have thought it all over carefully, I've no doubt that you will arrive at the same conclusion as I have.'

'And what's that?' demanded Stephens.

'The reason why Milton Vaizey was murdered,' answered Bill Groom, 'and the possible identity of his murderer.'

'Will I?' grunted Bluey with a grimace of disbelief. 'I'm not so sure. I haven't yet acquired the faculty of being able to see through a brick wall, like you have.'

Bill grinned. 'To see through a brick wall is impossible, old chap,' he remarked. 'But sometimes it's not very difficult to conjecture what's on the other side by looking at the objects that project above the wall.'

'When you start talking like that,' said Bluey disgustedly, 'I give up. As far as I can see, with regard to this particular brick wall, there's nothing above it, or round it, or underneath it to be seen at all, and all I do is bang my head against it until I get a headache!'

'There's an advantage even in that,' replied Bill, 'for if you bang hard enough you may eventually knock it down.'

He turned as Inspector Browne's voice boomed out, addressing him. 'There's nothing to be found here, Mr. Groom,' he said, coming towards them. 'There's ample evidence of someone having forced their way through the bushes, but not the slightest sign of a clue by which we can hope to trace who it was.'

'I didn't expect you would find anything,' said Groom.

'Of course,' continued the inspector, 'it's impossible to see very well by the light of a torch. I shall have another look in the daylight.'

'In the meanwhile,' said Bill, 'Stephens and I will be getting back to town; there's nothing more I can do at the moment. Is there a garage near here where I can hire a car?'

'There's one a stone's throw from the police station,' answered Browne. 'I'll walk as far with you, as I'm going back there.' He turned to the constable, who was standing stolidly behind him. 'You wait here, Jackson,' he ordered. 'Sergeant Paton will attend to the removal of the body.' The constable saluted, and they turned away.

'What are you going to do with Winter?' asked Bill as they left the scene of the tragedy and proceeded to walk towards the main road.

'I shall detain him pending further enquiries,' announced Inspector Browne.

'I'm not satisfied with his story, Mr. Groom, not satisfied at all.'

'I'm inclined to believe that he was speaking the truth,' said Bill. 'Anyway, it will be quite easy to verify. The copy of the marriage certificate can be looked up, and also his record at Scotland Yard.'

'That part of it may be true,' assented the inspector, 'and he possibly came to try and see his wife — but, hang it all, that doesn't mean he wasn't the person who broke into the library at The Priory.'

'In that case, what was his object?' said Groom. 'Why should he take the trouble to break in for the sole purpose of burning a lot of papers?'

'My opinion is that he expected to find something of value,' replied Browne, 'and destroyed the papers in a fit of temper when he found that there wasn't anything.'

'How do you know that there wasn't?' put in Dr. Compton. 'There might have been money in the safe.'

'That's possible, Doctor,' said the inspector. 'I shall have Winter searched. If, as I believe, he was caught in that trap while he was escaping, he wouldn't have had the opportunity to get rid of anything he had on him. I think I'll call back at The Priory now before going to the station and see.'

'I'm sure you will be wasting your time, Inspector,' murmured Bill. 'I'm positive that Winter had nothing whatever to do with the affair.'

'You may be right,' answered Browne, although the tone of his voice suggested that he considered it was most unlikely. 'At the same time, it can do no harm.'

They walked on in silence. Groom was fully occupied with his own thoughts, and Stephens took advantage of the lull in the conversation to turn over in his mind his friend's words of a few moments previously. It was evident that Bill in some way had managed to pierce through the veil of mystery that shrouded the darkness of Milton Vaizey and his secretary. His keen brain had apparently seized upon some clue that Bluey had missed — a clue that had supplied him with what he believed to be the solution of the problem.

The reporter ran over in his mind a brief résumé of the case. On the previous night Miss Bingham — Bluey couldn't think of her as Mrs. Winter — had been shot by a rifle bullet fired from the grounds of The Priory through the library window by some person, at present unknown.

The murderer had entered the grounds by way of the narrow lane and the orchard at the back, and was apparently familiar with the lay of the land, since he had cut the tripwires with which Vaizey had taken such elaborate precautions to guard himself against a surprise attack. Vaizey, at the time of his secretary's murder, had exhibited signs of intense fear; and according to his butler, he had for some time prior to his death been exceedingly uneasy, with the excuse that he was frightened of burglars. He had several times asked whether any person had been seen hanging about the estate after nightfall.

On the night following Miss Bingham's death he had been seen by Groom, and Bluey himself, stealthily leaving The

Priory after the household had all retired to bed, bound for a destination unknown. They had followed him and, on reaching Boulter's Wood near the main road, had heard the sound of two shots. Rushing forward, they had discovered that Vaizey had been shot dead, and a woman bending over his body with the revolver that had killed him in her hand. She had stated that a man whom she did not know had suddenly sprung out from some bushes and fired at Vaizey. She had refused to account for her own presence in the wood, but after a lot of persuasion had informed them that her name was Iris Wells.

In the breast pocket of Vaizey's jacket, Groom found a letter containing a warning and threats signed with the soubriquet of a blackmailer whose identity had baffled the police for months.

He had then returned to The Priory with Iris, to find that the place had been broken into and all the papers in the library destroyed. He had discovered half of a broken cufflink by the side of the open safe, and the sight of it had given

Iris Wells such a severe shock that it had rendered her unconscious and made her severely ill. Her father, Colonel Wells, who lived nearby, had said that neither he nor she knew Milton Vaizey, or had ever met the man. The safe apparently had been opened with the proper key, which Bill believed to have been in Vaizey's pocket at the time he was killed.

Later the same night, an ex-convict named Bert Winter, who said he was Miss Bingham's husband, had been caught in a man-trap while prowling about the grounds of The Priory.

These were the stray pieces of the puzzle, and Bluey tried vainly to fit them together in such a way that they formed a clear and connected whole. Bill had apparently succeeded in doing so; but the reporter, although he racked his brains until his head began to spin, had to admit that it was beyond him.

He was still worrying over it when they reached the gate of The Priory and took leave of Inspectors Browne, Bill promising to come down on the following day.

The first pale grey streaks of dawn were beginning to illuminate the eastern sky when the car they had hired from the garage at Esher drew to a halt at the door of Bluey's flat. The tired reporter climbed wearily out and, wishing Bill a sleepy good night, disappeared into the dark entrance of the building. Bill then directed the driver to take him to his own rooms.

Having paid the man, he let himself in and ascended the stairs to his sitting room. Slipping on a dressing gown, he mixed himself a drink and stood for some time staring thoughtfully at the dead ashes in the grate. Two things occupied his mind: who had killed Milton Vaizey and his secretary, and what was the exact position of Iris Wells regarding the whole affair? The thought of the woman predominated in spite of all his efforts to concentrate on the greater problem. It seemed almost incredible that twenty-four hours ago he had been completely oblivious of her existence, so thoroughly had she become a part of his life. It seemed to Bill as though he had always known her. It is like that with some people: so perfectly are they in tune with each other, that a lifetime of propinquity could not develop a more perfect understanding than they experienced at their first meeting.

Bill smiled, and his hand strayed to the place on his arm where Iris had rested her fingers during their walk from the wood to The Priory. He could almost feel the light touch of those fingers still.

With a muttered exclamation of impatience, he roused himself from his reverie and, lighting a cigar, flung himself into an armchair, resolutely deciding to put all thoughts of Iris out of his mind and devote himself to the mystery surrounding The Priory.

The hours sped by, and still he sat motionless. He might have been asleep, save for the occasional feather of blue smoke that curled upwards from the cigar gripped between his teeth.

It grew lighter outside as morning advanced, and streaks of pale yellow sunlight filtered through the half-drawn curtains; but still Bill remained, and so his housekeeper found him when she arrived with a broom and dustpan to clean the sitting room and lay the fire.

'Good gracious!' cried the startled woman as she caught sight of her employer. 'Have you been here all night?'

Bill rose, yawned, and stretched himself. 'Not all night, Mrs. Smith,' he replied. 'I didn't return home until early this morning.'

Mrs. Smith gave a snort of disgust. 'After criminals, as usual, I suppose,' she said, shaking her grey head. 'What I can't understand is why them people can't keep respectable hours like the rest of us — not that some of us do, I admit,' she added significantly

Bill laughed, and left the housekeeper to her labours. He felt half-dead from lack of sleep, and his eyes were hot and prickly; but a cold bath and a change of clothing almost restored him to his normal self. Breakfast was ready by the time he had dressed, and he did full justice to the meal.

Having left a message with Mrs. Smith for Bluey, in case he should ring up during his absence, Bill left his flat shortly after nine o'clock and soon passed under the big arch that gives entrance to Scotland Yard from Whitehall.

Hurrying to his office, he hastily glanced over the papers and reports that awaited him on his desk. Several required signing and, having hastily scrawled his signature to the more important of these, he pressed a bell on the desk. Of the sergeant who answered the summons, he enquired whether Inspector Martin had come in yet.

'He's in his office, sir, I think,' answered the man.

'Ask him to come and see me,' said Bill, 'and leave these with the assistant commissioner.' He pushed a little heap of papers across the desk, and the sergeant picked them up and hurried away.

After a minute or two there came a tap on the door, and in answer to Bill's invitation a tall, burly man entered.

It would have been impossible to have mistaken Inspector Martin for anything else but a policeman. From the tips of his large square-toed boots to the top of his bullet-shaped bristling head, he radiated 'detective'.

'Good morning, Martin,' said Bill with a smile, waving the inspector to a chair. 'Ever heard of The Ghost?' His eyes twinkled as he asked the question.

The inspector's rather pronounced eyes appeared in danger of falling out altogether. 'Have I ever heard of The Ghost!' he replied explosively. 'Haven't I spent the last eighteen months trying to find the fellow?'

'I thought you'd know about him,' said Bill, his smile broadening. 'I want you to let me have all the information you've got about him. I stumbled on something last night that brings him into the limelight again.' He briefly related to the astonished Martin the sequence of events that had occurred at The Priory on the previous night. 'I'm practically certain,' he finished, 'that The Ghost is not the murderer, but I'm certain he's at the bottom of the mystery.'

'How?' asked Martin.

'I'd rather not tell you at the moment,'

said Bill. 'It's only a theory, and I may be entirely wrong.'

Detective-Inspector Martin shrugged his broad shoulders. 'Just as you like,' he grunted. 'There's one thing that I'd like to ask you, though.'

'What's that?' said Bill.

'Have you any idea who The Ghost is?'

Bill pulled a box of cigarettes towards him and lit one, slowly expelled a cloud of smoke, and looked at the inspector. 'Yes,' he answered, 'I have a very good idea.'

Martin opened his mouth, but before he could speak Bill continued: 'Don't ask me to tell you any more at the moment. I promise you that you shall know everything as soon as I've got some proof. At the moment it's all guesswork.'

The inspector tugged furiously at his wiry moustache. 'That's all very well,' he grumbled, 'but I think you might at least tell me whom you suspect.'

Bill shook his head. 'I'll tell you when I've got absolute proof,' he repeated, 'and I hope to have that before the day's out.'

His words were prophetic, for before the sun rose again many things were to happen, and the mystery of The Priory was destined to be a mystery no longer.

'Well, I suppose I've got to be patient,' said Martin resignedly. 'I ought to be used to your peculiar ways by now.'

'Will you let me have all the notes you've got about The Ghost?' asked Bill.

'Yes, I'll send them in to you at once,' replied the inspector, rising to his feet and crossing to the door.

'Oh, and by the way,' said Bill, 'will you ask records for a list of all the unexplained suicides that have occurred during the past two years?'

'What in the world do you want that for?' asked the astonished inspector.

'Put it down to my peculiar ways,' chuckled Bill, and Martin left the room with an indignant grunt.

After he had gone, Bill crossed to the window and stood some time gazing out upon the Embankment. He loved the river, and would often stand and watch it flowing serenely past. It had a soothing effect on his mind. He wondered how Iris was. Looking at it sanely, it seemed to him one of the maddest things that had ever happened to him: that the whole of his thoughts should be occupied by a woman whom he had only met once, and then under conditions that should have been sufficient to preclude any vestige of the softer passions. And yet, there it was; try and disguise the fact as much as he would, it remained naked and starkly real. He loved Iris Wells. It was ridiculous, but it was the truth. He tried to analyse the reason and failed miserably. He had met many pretty women, and admired a few, but none of them had affected him as did this slip of a girl.

'Bill, old son, you're becoming a sentimental fool,' he muttered at length, and turned from the window to his desk as there came a tap on the door. A constable entered with two bulky folders. 'From Inspector Martin, sir,' he said, laying them on the desk.

Bill nodded a dismissal and the man withdrew. Lighting a fresh cigarette, and with a sigh that was not all weariness, though he felt tired out, Bill sat down. Spreading the contents of the folders in front of him, he commenced a close study of the typewritten sheets. An hour passed, and still Groom continued to wade patiently through the pile of papers, now and again making a brief note on the slip of paper at his side which he had put there for that purpose.

He had concluded his search among the records concerning the mysterious blackmailer, and was halfway through the list of suicides, when he uttered a sharp exclamation, and his fingers paused against a name that had suddenly caught his attention. He read the short paragraph that followed, and his eyes gleamed with elation. The mystery of Milton Vaizey's death was a mystery no longer, but its solution was a total surprise to Bill Groom.

# 12

## A Message from Esher

It was nearly lunchtime when Bill Groom left the Yard and made his way in the direction of the garage where he housed his powerful car. A few moments later he was running swiftly towards Stoke D'Abernon. After his discovery among the suicide records, he had spent a considerable time with Detective-Inspector Martin, and the result of their conversation had reduced that worthy to a state of amazement that was almost bordering on collapse.

As the car ran through Esher, it took Bill all his willpower to prevent himself from making a detour and stopping at The Beeches on the chance of being able to see Iris for a few moments to find out how she was getting on. But he had important work to do, and with a sigh of regret he passed the turning that would have taken him to the house, and sped on towards his destination.

It was a little after half-past two when he brought the car to a halt at the entrance to Sir Bryan Walsh's house and, descending from the driver's seat, hurried up the steps and rang the bell. A few seconds later he was shaking hands with the scientist.

'Well, Bill, you're the last person I expected to see,' said the tall grey-haired man as he pushed forward a chair.

'I didn't expect to be here myself,' Bill replied. 'As a matter of fact, you can help me.'

'I will do anything I can, of course,' answered Sir Bryan. 'What is it all about?' He pushed forward a box of cigars, and Bill, lighting one of the fragrant weeds, settled himself in the chair.

'It's a matter of murder,' he answered. 'And it concerns a whole lot of people, but particularly a woman in whom I am rather interested.'

'I see,' answered the scientist. 'I'm intrigued. Tell me all about it.'

Bill briefly outlined the case, and he

told his story so well that Sir Bryan was able to form a clear picture of the scene and the characters who had peopled the drama.

'Well, Bill,' he remarked, when the young superintendent concluded, 'of all the cases you've ever told me about, this one's the strangest. I must congratulate you on the way in which you have pieced the puzzle together.'

'I haven't pieced it together quite yet,' replied Bill. 'The completion of it rests with you.'

'Well, come up to my laboratory, and we'll get on with the work without delay. It shouldn't take long.'

Sir Bryan crossed to the door and held it open for his companion to pass through. 'By the way,' he said as they ascended the staircase together, 'do you think the woman's illness is likely to be serious?'

'No,' replied Bill. 'I believe it's more nerves than anything else, and I am hoping that the news I shall be able to take to The Beeches will completely cure her.'

'Don't forget to send me an invitation to the wedding,' said the scientist with a chuckle as he paused outside a green baize door and searched in his pocket for the key.

Bill reddened. 'You're rather rushing things, aren't you?' he said. 'I only met her last night.'

'There's no such thing as time, Bill,' laughed Sir Bryan, unlocking the door. 'Any scientist will tell you that.'

He passed into the room beyond, followed by his companion. It was a long, lofty room with whitewashed walls, lit by an overhead skylight. Down the centre ran a glass-topped table. One wall was completely covered by shelves laden with countless bottles and strangely shaped glass instruments.

Sir Bryan Walsh relocked the door and switched on the powerful lights that hung suspended over the experimental table. He crossed to a row of bookshelves and, taking down a thick volume, turned to a certain page and handed it to Bill; then, unlocking a glass-fronted cupboard, he brought out a high-powered microscope which he set on the table. From the same cupboard he took a box of blank slides and, selecting three, placed them beside the microscope.

Asking Bill for the little seed envelope in which he had put the blood-stained shred of leather, he shook out the contents into a smaller glass dish. The blood on it was dry and hard by now, and with the aid of a small knife Walsh managed to scrape some off into a watch-glass. It had the appearance of brownish dust, somewhat resembling rust. Having obtained sufficient for his purpose, the scientist reached up to a shelf above the table and took down a bottle labelled Pure Alcohol. He removed the stopper and with the aid of a pipette drew out some of the volatile liquid, allowing a few drops to fall upon the dried blood in the watch-glass.

Bill watched interestedly while he stirred it gently with a platinum needle, and presently the hard particles began to dissolve in the potent spirit, colouring it a brownish-red. At last, when it was mixed to his satisfaction, Sir Bryan took up one of the blank slides and placed a single drop from the end of the needle, smearing it out until it formed a thin film. Laying this on the table, he crossed over to the shelves and returned with a small bottle labelled Methylene Blue. With this he coloured the film on the glass slide and covered it with a cover-glass, securing it in its place by means of two rubber bands.

He repeated this operation with the other two slides; and then, adjusting the light so that it fell full upon the mirror of the microscope, he laid one of the slides upon the stage and peered through the eyepiece, his fingers turning the milled brass screw at the side until the focus was correct.

For some moments he remained bending over the instrument while Bill watched him intently. Presently a little grunt of satisfaction escaped the scientist. Straightening up, he consulted the book that lay open on the table by his side, and then turning once more to the microscope he carefully examined in the same way the other two slides that he had made. He turned to Bill.

'You were right,' he said. 'There's no getting away from it. It proves beyond any shadow of a doubt the identity of the person who killed Mr. Vaizey and his secretary.'

Bill nodded. 'I thought it would,' he replied. 'I'm glad in a way — and I'm sorry, too, if you understand what I mean.'

The scientist laid his hand on his shoulder. 'I can understand what you mean, Bill,' he said.

They remained talking for some time, and then Bill excused himself and took his departure. He drove to his own flat, and his first action on reaching home was to sit down at his desk and write a letter. It was a short letter, and having completed it and sealed it in an envelope, he addressed it to 'Colonel Wells, The Beeches, Esher'. Calling Mrs. Smith, he gave it to her to post, and, lighting a cigarette, stared thoughtfully out of the window.

As the scientist had said, his case was complete, but there was still a lot to consider before he took action. It was a complicated business, and Bill felt little relish for the task that his sense of duty to the community at large forced him to perform.

The afternoon faded into evening, and the room grew darker as the daylight outside slowly disappeared. His duty was plain, but Bill shirked the inevitable result that would accrue when the hand of the law was set in motion. It was impossible that he had made a mistake, for everything pointed to the fact that he was right. He had proved it up to the hilt. There was no getting away from the evidence of the microscope. Taken in conjunction with the other facts, it was proof positive — and yet Bill wished with all his heart that he was wrong. But two lives had been taken, and by all the laws of man and nature, the person responsible must pay the penalty.

A coal fell from the grate, and the noise, striking suddenly upon the silence of the room, roused him from his thoughts, and he turned with a start. At the same moment there came a ring at the front-door bell, and a second later Bluey came cheerily into the room.

'Hello, old man,' he greeted Bill. 'Where have you been all day? I've called twice.'

'I've been over to see Walsh, Bluey,' answered Bill. 'To forge the last link in the Vaizey case.'

'The last link!' echoed Bluey. 'Do you mean that you have solved the problem?'

'Yes,' replied Bill. 'It's all over, bar shouting. I not only know who killed Vaizey and his secretary, but I also know the identity of The Ghost.'

'Who is it, old man?' asked the reporter eagerly.

Bill leant against the mantelpiece. 'The Ghost — ' he began, and the telephone bell rang sharply and instantly. 'Excuse me,' he said, and crossed to the instrument. 'Hello! Yes — speaking. Who is that?' There was a long pause, and then: 'All right, I'll come right away now . . . Yes, tell him at once.' He hung up the black cylinder and swung round to address the reporter. 'Phone up the garage, Bluey, there's a good chap, and ask them to send the car round immediately.'

'What's happened?' his friend asked curiously.

'Robert Trevor has had a serious heart attack and is not expected to live,' snapped Bill. 'He wants to see me urgently. Hurry, old son!'

He switched on the electric light as he spoke, and Bluey, turning to the telephone, saw that his friend's face was tense with excitement.

Bill hurried into the adjoining room while Bluey got through to the garage. When he returned he was clad in a heavy motor coat.

'The car will be here in a few seconds,' said Bluey. 'I say, what's it all about, Bill? You haven't — '

'There's no time to answer questions now, old chap,' Bill interrupted. 'We've got to get down to Esher as quickly as possible.'

He watched impatiently at the window for the arrival of the car, and presently it glided up to the kerb. They left the entrance to the flats, and Bill took the place of the mechanic who had brought the machine round. Without a wasted second, they started on the journey.

Once clear of the London streets, Bill let the powerful car all out, and it flew along the country road at a speed that made Bluey cling to his seat to save himself from being thrown out. Conversation was impossible, for Bill's attention was concentrated on the road ahead, and the reporter, although he was consumed with curiosity, was forced to keep silent.

In an incredibly short space of time they reached the outskirts of Esher, and presently swinging into the Oxshott Road, stopped outside the gate of The Homestead. Bill sprang out almost before the car had stopped and, followed by Bluey, hurried up the little path to the front door. The arrival of the car had evidently been heard, for before he could raise his hand to the knocker the door opened and the manservant who had admitted Bill before ushered them into the hall. He looked white and anxious, and in answer to Bill's question pointed up the stairs.

'The master's in bed, sir,' he said in a trembling voice. 'Dr. Compton's with him. He was taken bad all of a sudden.' He led the way up the stairs while he talked, and paused before a door on the landing. Tapping on this, he opened it, and stood aside to let Bill and his friend enter.

The room was plainly furnished as a bedroom; and in the bed, which occupied the centre, lay the figure of the old explorer. His face was pale, and round his eyes were large blue circles. He looked thinner, too, than when Bill had seen him before.

'It's good of you to come so promptly,' he said in a thin, feeble voice as the young superintendent approached the bedside. 'Perhaps, Dr. Compton, you wouldn't mind leaving us for a few minutes. I have something of the utmost importance to communicate privately to Mr. Groom.'

Dr. Compton rose from the chair on which he had been seated on the other side of the bed. 'Certainly,' he said. 'I'll be downstairs if you want me.' He nodded to

Bill and left the room, closing the door behind him.

'Who — who is that with you?' asked the old man, looking at Bluey.

'It is only a friend of mine,' replied Bill gently. 'You can speak quite freely before him.'

Robert Trevor closed his eyes for a moment. 'What I'm going to say,' he managed after a little pause, 'will come as a great shock to you.'

'I don't think it will,' answered Bill. 'I think I know already.'

The old man's eyes opened wide, and he stared. 'You — you know!' he whispered in a voice that was scarcely audible.

Bill nodded.

'But you can't know,' said Trevor, trying to struggle up on to one elbow. 'What I want to tell you is this: it was I who killed Miss Bingham and Milton Vaizey!'

# 13

## The Ghost

Bill Groom bent over the old man and, taking him gently by the shoulders, laid him back upon the pillow. The exertion had proved almost too much for Trevor, and after his startling announcement he lay back with closed eyes, breathing heavily and jerkily. Bill looked round and motioned to Bluey to hand him a glass of water that stood on a small table by the bedside. The old man sipped it gratefully as Bill supported him on his arm and held it to his lips. It was some time before he was able to speak again.

'Yes, I killed them,' he murmured faintly at length.

'I know,' said Bill. 'I knew before you told me.'

An expression of surprise crept into Robert Trevor's eyes. 'How did you know?' he asked. 'How long have you known?'

'I have known for certain since this afternoon,' Bill replied. 'I suspected from the time Vaizey was shot.'

'I received a great shock when I learned from you that that poor woman was dead,' said the old man. 'I never meant to injure her.'

'It was a mistake, wasn't it?' said Bill. 'I thought it might have been.'

Trevor moved restlessly. 'It was a terrible mistake,' he answered in a broken voice. 'It has preyed on my mind ever since. I would give anything in the world to undo that, but I'd no idea she was even in the house. I thought she'd gone away on her usual visit; it was the date.'

'And you mistook her for Vaizey,' prompted Bill.

'Yes; from where I fired I could only see her dimly. If I'd known that she had not been away, I should have been more careful.'

'Why did you shoot Vaizey?' asked Bill, bending nearer, for Robert Trevor's voice was so low and tremulous that it was difficult to hear what he said.

The old man's eyes suddenly blazed

with an expression of intense hatred. 'I shot Vaizey because he was one of the vilest men who ever drew breath — because he was a murderer!' he answered. 'A heartless, inhuman scoundrel. I do not regret in the least that I killed him, for I believe that I rendered the civilised world a service. I would do the same again tomorrow!'

'I think that you had better tell me the whole story, if you feel strong enough,' suggested Bill gently.

Trevor nodded weakly. 'It is my intention to do so,' he replied. 'That's why I asked you to come here.'

'My friend can take down any statement you make,' said Bill. 'And if you will sign it in our presence, we can act as witnesses. Of course, should you recover, I'm afraid that . . . ' He fell silent, unwilling to finish his sentence.

'I shall not recover,' said the old man. 'After all, it's better this way. I have done what I set out to do, and I regret nothing except that dreadful mistake. Poor Miss Bingham.' He paused and moistened his dry lips. 'If you're ready,' he continued, 'I will begin.'

Bill beckoned to Bluey to come closer, and the reporter seated himself on the edge of the bed and produced a notebook and pencil. There was a short silence while Trevor lay with closed eyes, evidently thinking how to begin. After a few seconds he opened them and looked at Bill.

'I will be as brief as possible,' he began jerkily. 'I am a widower. It is now nearly seven years since my wife died. She passed away at our house in Devonshire while I was abroad on a trip that took me into the interior of west Africa. I hurried home as soon as I received the news that she was ill, but it had taken a considerable time to reach me, and when I arrived it was to find that I was over a fortnight too late.

'I wasn't even in time to attend the funeral, for that, of course, had taken place a week before I landed in England. There was a son born of our marriage, and he was with his mother to the last. He had been sent for from college, for at the time of her death he was just seventeen. You may think this is all irrelevant, but you'll see presently that it is necessary for you to understand everything.'

He paused to recover his breath, and Bill stooped to wipe away the beads of perspiration that had broken out on the old man's forehead.

'I swore at the time,' Trevor went on, 'that I would never go away again; but after two years the wanderlust got me once more in its grip. The house was full of memories, and I decided to sell it. My son, Chris, was still away completing his education, and before leaving England I arranged with my solicitors to make him a quarterly allowance which I considered sufficient for his needs. It was my intention to take one more trip and then settle down with my boy who, by that time, would have left the university.

'All that occurred later I feel was my fault, for if I had stayed at home to look after him, it would never have happened. The expedition took longer than anticipated, for we had ill luck all the time. Our bearers suffered from severe attacks of relapsing fever and sleeping sickness, which are very prevalent in that part of the world, and died like flies. I myself was stricken with the fever, and for months lay in state of unconsciousness. To add to our troubles, we got lost in the jungle, and our food ran out. The man who had accompanied me had died from sleeping sickness, and I was eventually left with but one old native bearer — a faithful fellow who had served me several of my previous trips.

'It is a waste of time to go into all the details. Suffice it to say that it was three years before I again saw the land of my birth, and when I returned — broken in health and a wreck of my former self — a terrible shock awaited me.

'Naturally, the first person I enquired for was son, and I learned that he had committed suicide.'

Bluey looked up quickly and met Bill's eye. He was beginning to understand at last.

'From the solicitors I found out as much of the truth as was known,' Robert Trevor continued. 'It seemed that two years after my departure abroad, Chris left Oxford and came up to London. He took a furnished flat just off Piccadilly, and then the trouble started. He got in with a bad set, began drinking and gambling, and lived at a rate that was far above even the ample means that I had left at his disposal. At last he found it was impossible to carry on; he was at the end of his resources and being pressed by his creditors on every side.

'Among the men of his acquaintance was one who was reputed to be exceedingly wealthy and beginning to acquire something of a reputation in the City for his daring speculations on the stock exchange. Chris approached him and tried to borrow the necessary money to save himself from ruin. His request was met with refusal, and in desperation the boy forged the name of this man as the acceptor of a bill drawn in favour of himself. The man's name was Milton Vaizey.'

The old man stopped for a second. His strength was clearly at the last ebb, and it was only by a supreme effort of will that he forced himself to go on.

'The forgery was never questioned,' he recommenced, clearing his throat, 'and the bill was discounted. With the proceeds Chris was enabled to pay the most pressing of his debts, and for a time his troubles were at an end. A few weeks after, however, came the bombshell. My son received a letter stating the forgery was known to the writer, and that unless he was prepared to pay a large sum, the truth concerning it would be placed before Milton Vaizey. The letter was typewritten, and signed 'The Ghost'.

'It sent Chris into a fit of panic. He had no means of finding the amount the blackmailer demanded and, foreseeing the difficulties that would result from exposure, he shot himself.'

Trevor's voice broke huskily in his throat. He continued tremulously: 'I learned these facts from the letter that Chris wrote just before his death and sent to me care of the solicitors. In it he confessed the whole story, and the anguish of his tortured mind is clearly revealed.

'When I read that last pitiful letter, I took a solemn oath that I would never rest until I had discovered the man who had driven Chris to his death — the cowardly scoundrel who cloaked his identity beneath the alias The Ghost, and who was as morally guilty as though he had shot the boy with his own hand.

'My intentions when I had found him I never disguised from myself for an instant. I intended to kill him with as little compunction as I would have killed a wild beast. He had taken from me all I held dear in the world — my son — and I was prepared to devote the whole of my life if necessary to avenge the boy's death.

'I realised at the outset that I had set myself a difficult task; I had nothing to work from — not the slightest clue that might lead me to the writer of that letter. I could not take anyone into my confidence without disclosing the truth concerning the forgery, and at all costs that had to be suppressed for the sake of Chris's name.

'My first action, naturally, was to visit the people who had discounted the bill in order to take it up, and so prevent it from reaching the hands of Milton Vaizey, who would, of course, have immediately learned of the forgery. Here I received a second shock. Although the bill had still six months to go before it fell due, it had already been redeemed, and the person who had redeemed it was Milton Vaizey himself. That made me think, particularly when I found on further enquiries that he had done so about a week before Chris had received the fatal letter from The Ghost.

'This man, Vaizey, whom I had never met, and knew nothing about, must have been aware for some time that his acceptance of the bill was a forgery. Why, therefore, had he remained silent? Why had he not come forward and confronted Chris with the fact that he knew? It was impossible to believe that it was out of friendship for the boy. He had never been more than a mere acquaintance, and if he had been inclined to help Chris, he would have lent him the money in the first instance. There must have been some other motive for his silence, and as I thought the matter over, a suspicion began to form in my mind that Milton Vaizey was The Ghost.'

Two high spots of colour had appeared in the old man's cheeks. His voice grew stronger under the influence of the excitement. Bill realised, however, from his laboured breathing that it was temporary, and that at any moment the relapse that was bound to follow might take place.

As Trevor paused for breath, Bill saw that there was a bottle of brandy on a cabinet in a corner of the room. Rising to his feet, he crossed over to it and poured a small quantity of its contents into a wine glass that stood by the side. Returning to the bedside, he held the glass to the old man's lips. 'Drink some of this,' he said gently.

Trevor sipped a little of the spirit. 'Thank you,' he murmured gratefully. 'I'm afraid that my narrative must seem rather long, but I want to place you in possession of all the facts. There is not much more to tell.'

Bill set the glass down on the table, and

the old man went on: 'Of course, I had no proof that my idea was correct, but from that time I began to make cautious enquiries concerning Vaizey. No one seemed to know much about him, or where he had obtained his money, although it was an established fact that he was a fairly wealthy man. But try as I might, I could learn nothing to support my suspicions. Vaizey had bought a house near Esher called The Priory, and in order to be able to watch him the more closely, I came to live here.

'I think that some of my enquiries concerning him reached his ears, for shortly after my arrival he began to take the precautions of which you are aware, and surrounded The Priory with a number of man-traps and tripwires. He was, no doubt, aware that I was Chris's father, and my proximity gave him cause for alarm. He was afraid of me, and of what I might know. Although I had no proof, I was certain in my own mind that he was The Ghost.

'For weeks I watched him, hoping to get the proof I required. With that intention I made the acquaintance of Miss Bingham on the chance of being able to find out something of Vaizey's private affairs; but here again, I met with no result. Miss Bingham never spoke about herself or her employer, and in spite of my most careful questions I could discover absolutely nothing. My determination, however, never weakened for one moment; if it ever had any tendency to, the sight of my dead boy's last letter, which I always kept by me, would have been sufficient to hold me to my purpose. I knew that if my revenge were to be carried out at all, it must be done soon — for already I had had several warnings that my heart was in a serious condition, and I was aware that at any moment I might succumb to one of the attacks which were becoming more frequent.

'I began to watch The Priory. The tripwires and other devices that Vaizey had laid down offered no serious obstacle. I knew of their existence, and it did not take me long to discover the exact position of each, after which they were no longer a source of danger to me. From nightfall until the early hours of the morning I used to lie concealed in the grounds at a point from where I could command a view of both the back and the front exits. After little more than a week, my vigilance and patience were rewarded.

'One night shortly after twelve o'clock, I saw Vaizey leave the house by the front entrance and make his way swiftly down the drive. I followed, but on that occasion I lost him in Boulter's Wood. Three days later, however, I saw him start on another nocturnal excursion, and this time I managed to track him to his destination. To my surprise, this turned out to be The Beeches — Colonel Wells's house, the back of which is approached through the wood.'

The old man paused again and Bluey looked up at Bill, opening his mouth as though to speak, but at a frown from his friend remained silent. The whole tangled skein was becoming clear. He bent once more to his notes as Trevor began again.

'Vaizey made his way across the grounds, and from thence round to the front entrance. I followed and, watching him from a patch of shrubbery, saw him take a letter from his pocket and push it under the front door. Had there been a letter-box into which he could have dropped it, I might never have discovered absolutely and without any shadow of a doubt that Vaizey and The Ghost were one and the same.

'After delivering the letter, Vaizey retreated furtively, and started to return the way he had come. I let him go without bothering to follow, for I was certain that what I wanted to know was contained in the letter he had just pushed under the door. It was no ordinary communication from one neighbour to another; the stealthy way in which it had been delivered convinced me of that. The question was, how was I to get a look at it?

'I am an old campaigner, and after a moment's thought a method suggested itself. Near the shrubbery where I lay concealed was an arch of galvanised iron wire supporting rambler roses. I broke off a piece of this wire, about eighteen inches long. Bending the end into a hook, I went up to the door and inserted the wire beneath it. I fished about gently, and at the end of two or three vain attempts I succeeded in locating the letter, and gradually drew it towards me from under the door. I could not very well stop to examine it there, so put it in my pocket and hurried home as quickly as I could.

'Once in the privacy of my own room, I eagerly took it from my pocket. The envelope bore the inscription 'Colonel Wells, Urgent' scrawled across it, and for a second I hesitated before opening it. Then, believing that the end justified the means, I quickly thrust aside my momentary scruple, and ripping open the envelope, took out the contents, a single sheet of paper. It only required one glance at the signature to show me that my suspicions had been well-founded. I had succeeded in my quest. I knew beyond doubt the name of the man who had been the cause of my son's death. I can remember every word of that letter as well as if I had it before me. It was quite brief, but the few lines conveyed the whole story. It ran: 'The last amount you paid was not enough; I must have more. If you fail, you know what to expect. The Ghost.' And Milton Vaizey was The Ghost!

'The excitement of my discovery brought on a heart attack, and for two days I was unable to leave the house. But during those two days' enforced confinement, I planned my campaign. I knew that Vaizey was in the habit of spending his evenings in the library, for I had often seen him at work at his writing table in the course of my long watch on The Priory. I am an excellent shot, and I decided that I would shoot him from the vantage of the shrubbery at the end of the lawn.'

Robert Trevor turned his head slowly on the pillow, and regarded Bill with eyes that seemed to have sunk further into his thin face. He seemed to find difficulty in breathing.

'The night, as you know, was well-suited to my purpose, for there was not a soul abroad. I took the precaution of cutting the tripwires in case it was necessary for a hasty escape, and made my way to the point I had selected as being the best from which to obtain a view of the library window. Vaizey was already seated at the table — or so I imagined then — and, carefully taking aim, I fired. I waited to assure myself that the shot had been true, and then I hurried home as fast as I could.

'I tore my hand while getting over the barbed wire fence at the end of the orchard, but I didn't realise it until I was safely back in my own study. I was elated, exultant! I had destroyed the man who had destroyed my boy. My son's death was avenged!

'You can imagine the terrible shock I received when later that night you arrived and informed me that it was Miss Bingham whom I had killed, and not Milton Vaizey, after all! Can you wonder that I fainted? I had taken an innocent life! I was a murderer! I never considered the act of killing Milton Vaizey would be a murder. To me it was purely justice. I can honestly say that the worst ordeal of my life was when I had to answer your questions, while my brain was a seething chaos. I kept my right hand clenched so that you wouldn't notice the gash in the palm, and when you and the inspector had gone I set myself to thinking out my next move.

'I was still determined to carry out my original intention, and after a considerable amount of thought I decided that the only way was to continue my watch on Vaizey, and try and get him when he was off his guard.

'I knew that he would regard the death of his secretary as an accident and be fully aware that it was in reality an attempt against his own life; therefore there was little chance of his exposing himself to a similar attack. I was confident that he was aware at this time who was at the bottom of it, but I also knew that he dared not say anything without giving himself away.

'The opportunity that I sought came sooner than I expected. On the following night, armed with a loaded revolver, I once more started my vigil at The Priory; and when you and your friend — for I suppose it was he — followed Vaizey to

Boulter's Wood, I was close behind you. My experience in the African jungle had taught me the art of stalking without betraying my presence. As soon as Vaizey made for the footpath I knew where he was going, and when once I had reached the cover of the trees I hurried ahead, making a wide detour so that I could head him off. The risk was a big one, because I knew that you were close behind; but so long as I achieved my purpose I cared little whether I was caught or not.

'Reaching the clearing, I concealed myself in a patch of bushes and waited for Vaizey to approach. As he drew nearer, I became aware of someone else approaching in the opposite direction, but I never troubled to see who it was. My whole mind was concentrated on the man whom I now had completely at my mercy. As he drew level with the bushes, I sprang out at him and fired twice, full in his face. In the light of the flashes I just caught the expression of fearful terror that convulsed his features before he fell, and a wave of satisfaction passed through me. Someone screamed at that moment, and I dropped the pistol and fled. That is all!'

Trevor sank back among his pillows breathlessly, for in his excitement he had raised himself on one elbow. 'I feel no remorse, except in the case of poor Miss Bingham, for what I have done.'

Bill was silent; he felt that there was little to say.

The old man closed his eyes and lay back completely exhausted, the breath hissing through his clenched teeth in irregular pants.

Bill reached for and took Bluey's notebook from his hand. 'If you will sign this,' he said, bending over the bed, 'my friend and I will attach our signatures.'

Trevor opened his eyes and nodded feebly, and Bill could see that with the relaxing of the willpower that had kept him up during the relating of his confession, the thin thread of life was rapidly running out. Placing his arm about the old man's shoulders he raised him up, and Bluey put his fountain pen in the shaking hand. Trevor scrawled his signature, and Bluey and Bill added theirs. They had scarcely done so when Bill felt a sudden spasm contracting the thin body. Trevor's face went livid, and he strove vainly to get his breath.

'Quick, Bluey!' said Bill. 'Call Dr. Compton!'

The reporter ran to the door, and opening it, shouted loudly into the passage. There came a sound of hurried footsteps on the stairs, and Compton rushed up, but he was too late. Even as he entered the room, Bill felt the body he was supporting go suddenly limp. There was a little rattling sound in Trevor's throat, and Bill laid him gently down.

'He has gone on his last expedition,' he said quietly.

# 14

## The Last Mystery

The following morning broke bright and clear, the slight touch of frost in the air adding a tang that was not altogether unpleasant, as Bill, accompanied by Bluey, swung the car out of Oxford Street and sent it travelling once more in the direction of Esher.

After Robert Trevor's confession and death the previous night, Bill had called at the police station and acquainted the astonished and amazed Inspector Browne of the full details of the story. Leaving him almost incoherent at the news, Bill had then returned home in search of a well-earned rest, for he had had little sleep during the past two days.

Immediately after breakfast he had rung up Bluey, asking his friend to call for him at Scotland Yard, and had announced his intention of returning to Esher to gather up a few remaining threads that were left loose.

Only one mystery remained to be solved, and Bill had a pretty good idea regarding the solution; but before he could call the case finished, it had to be tested and proved. With this object in view, he and the reporter were now speeding along the deserted country roads bound for The Beeches, where he hoped the final unravelling of the tangled skein would take place.

It was a delicate mission, and Bill was not looking forward to his task at all. During the journey he turned over in his mind the best way of conducting his interview with the colonel. As he drew nearer to Esher, his thoughts wandered from the problem, and he began to think about Iris. Would he be able to get a glimpse of her? he wondered. He was hoping so, and once again was astonished at himself for taking so much interest in a woman who was little more than a stranger. Yet it seemed to Bill as if he had known her for years — had always known her. He wondered if she hated him because of his apparent callousness when he had found her in the wood. Or did she realise that he had only been doing his duty? Bill sighed and wished the suspense were over.

He was still wondering when he brought the car to a standstill in front of the Gothic porch that formed the main entrance to The Beeches, and slipping from the driver's seat, tugged at the wrought-iron bell-pull.

'I want to see Colonel Wells on a matter of business,' he said, handing his card to the staid and venerable servant who answered the summons.

The man eyed him respectfully for a second, and then, in a hushed voice that implied by its tone that he was conferring a tremendous favour on the visitors, invited Bill and Bluey into the spacious hall. Producing a salver with the air of a magician, and laying the card upon it, he bore it away and vanished through a door at the end of the hall.

Bill allowed his gaze to wander round him, and nodded appreciatively. The old oak furniture and staircase, black with age; the suits of armour and tapestries; the carved stonework and leaded windows, all gave to the whole place an atmosphere of the mediaeval — an atmosphere that was strangely restful and peaceful.

After a short interval the manservant returned and informed them in mild surprise that Colonel Wells would see them in a moment. He had scarcely delivered this message when Wells himself entered the hall and advanced to meet Bill with an outstretched hand.

'Good morning,' he said genially. 'What do you wish to see me about?' He looked enquiringly at Bluey.

'There are one or two things I should like to talk over with you,' said Bill, shaking hands and introducing the reporter.

'Come up to the library,' said the colonel, and led the way up the oak staircase. He ushered them into a room on the right of a wide landing and pushed forward a couple of easy chairs.

'How's your daughter?' asked Bill as he sat down. The question had been hovering on his lips from the moment he entered the house.

The colonel's face clouded. 'She has recovered consciousness,' he answered, 'but she's still far from well. I am expecting Dr. Compton at any moment; he promised to come again first thing this morning, but hasn't turned up yet.'

'Do you think that I could see her?' said Bill.

'I've no objection, if the doctor will permit it,' answered the colonel. 'Provided, of course, that you don't say anything likely to upset her.'

'I shan't do that,' said Bill. 'What I have to say to her will, I think, go a long way towards restoring her to health.'

The colonel looked at him quickly. 'I don't understand you,' he said.

'Colonel Wells,' said Bill, nerving himself for the ordeal which he had been dreading, 'I want to ask you a plain question, not as a police officer, but as a friend. What was your object in breaking into The Priory on the night Vaizey was shot?'

Colonel Wells dropped his cigar and let it smoulder unheeded on the carpet. His hands clenched until the knuckles stood out white, and his face paled under its habitual tan. 'What do you mean?' he asked huskily.

'I'm right, am I not?' said Bill. 'It was you, wasn't it?'

'Yes, it was me.' The answer came in a low, strangled voice as though each word almost choked the man who uttered them. 'Though how the devil you know, I can't guess.'

'I know a lot of things,' said Bill. 'For instance, I know that you went there to try and recover a document or documents held by Milton Vaizey that compromised you in some way. Is that not so?'

The colonel remained silent.

'We have already discovered that Vaizey was a blackmailer well-known to the Yard,' Groom continued, 'who carried on his nefarious trade under the name of The Ghost.'

'You — you know that!' exclaimed Wells.

Bill nodded. 'That, and a lot more. The mystery surrounding Vaizey's death has been cleared up. We know who killed him and why. The murderer confessed last night.'

The colonel gave an exclamation, and a shadow seemed to lift from his face. 'Is that true?' he asked, and his voice was lighter and less strained, as though a great weight had lifted from his mind.

'Perfectly true,' said Bill. 'The statement witnessed by myself and my friend is at present at Scotland Yard.'

'Who was it? Who killed him?' enquired Wells.

'Robert Trevor,' answered Bill.

'Good God!' exclaimed Wells in amazement. 'And I thought — ' He broke off quickly.

'You thought,' said Bill, eyeing him steadily, 'that it was your daughter who had killed Vaizey — and she was under the impression that it was you!'

'Yes, you're quite right,' muttered the colonel in a low voice. 'I did think it might have been Iris.' He paused for a moment doubtfully, and then continued: 'As you seem to have guessed so much, perhaps I had better tell you the whole story.'

'I think it would be as well,' Bill agreed. 'I can assure you, Colonel, that so long as it does not interfere with the course of justice — and I don't see in this case how it can very well, since the only two persons concerned are both dead — whatever you tell me I shall treat in the strictest confidence.'

The colonel inclined his head and, walking across to the window, gazed out. Presently he came back to the centre of the room and, resting his hands on the table, cleared his throat. 'What I am about to tell you,' he began, 'is known only to one other person — my daughter. It was known to a third, but he is now dead.

'Many years ago, when I was a young man, and before I met the lady who afterwards became my wife, I fell violently in love with a woman much younger than I; I was thirty at the time. It was really, as I soon discovered, nothing but a mad infatuation, and in any case it could never have led to anything; for the woman in question — for obvious reasons I cannot divulge her name — was married. A number of foolish letters passed between us. There was nothing in them really, but they were indiscreet, and could easily have been construed to mean more than they did.

'When I married eventually, I believed that these letters had been destroyed. I was later to be assured that they had not. By some means or other they got into the hands of the most pitiless and inhuman scoundrel that ever lived. I think that they must have been stolen by a valet of mine whom I had occasion to discharge for some petty thefts. However, it is immaterial how they reached the hands of The Ghost; it is sufficient that they did so.

'About eight months ago I received a letter that had been pushed under the door one night, stating that the writer was in possession of these letters and offering me the alternative of paying five thousand pounds, or of having the letters made public. I am not a rich man, but the thought of the result of that stupid correspondence reaching the hands of the husband of the lady who had written them caused me to pay. I knew that he was a very jealous and suspicious man, and would in all probability create a scandal that might possibly end in divorce. For the sake of the woman, I could do no less than prevent that at all costs.

'The money was to be paid in Treasury notes and forwarded to the post office at Charing Cross for collection in the name of Roberts. The Ghost informed me in the letter that if I went to the police or in any way tried to trace the person who called at the post office, the letters would instantly be sent to the husband of the woman concerned.

'That first payment was one of many, and I began to dread coming down in the morning for fear of finding the familiar letter with further demands on my resources awaiting me. My income had already been swallowed up, and I had begun to encroach on my capital. I foresaw ruin ahead unless by some means I could put a stop to the persecution of this blackmailer. I had taken my daughter into my confidence, and her advice was to let him do his worst and go to the police, but I was thinking of the effect any publicity would have upon the woman whose present happiness would undoubtedly be destroyed. I knew that she was very highly strung and neurotic, and that at the slightest breath of scandal she might quite conceivably take her own life. The suicide of a well-known society woman that had been laid at the door of The Ghost was then occupying a good deal of space in the papers, and added to my fears.

'One night, quite by accident, a way out of my difficulties presented itself. I was suffering from a slight attack of indigestion, and being unable to sleep I made up my mind to come down to the library for a book I had been reading earlier in the evening. Rising from my bed, I slipped on a dressing gown, and by chance happened to look out of the window. My bedroom faces the front of the house, and it was a bright, clear, moonlit night. As I glanced out I saw a shadowy figure come stealthily round the corner of the house and approach the porch. At first I thought it was a burglar, but presently as I watched, the moon illuminated the man's face, and I saw with surprise that it was Milton Vaizey, the owner of The Priory. I had seen him once or twice before in Esher, and was sure that I was not mistaken.

'It was long past twelve, and I wondered what on earth he could be doing at The Beeches at that hour, but even then no suspicion of the real truth entered my mind. I hurried down the stairs with the intention of finding out what he wanted, and as I entered the hall I saw something white appear under the door. I picked it up, and found that it was another communication from the blackmailer, and then the significance of Vaizey's presence at the house at that hour of the night burst upon me. He was The Ghost!

'I was so overcome with amazement and surprise that for several minutes I stood unable to move; and when at last I opened the front door and looked out, all was silent and still. The man had gone.

'I thought the matter over that night, and the next morning I told Iris of my discovery. She was as much amazed as I, and suggested that I should at once inform the police. But the same difficulty regarding that still stood in the way. Besides, during the night I had evolved a plan which was no less than to break into The Priory and try, if possible, to recover the letters.'

Colonel Wells paused for a moment and puffed at his cigar, which he had retrieved from the carpet. Bill looked at him with a gleam of admiration in his eyes. Few men would have borne so much persecution for the sake of chivalrously defending a woman's name.

'Iris did everything in her power to try and dissuade me,' the colonel continued, 'but I had made up my mind. On the night that Milton Vaizey was killed I set out to put my plan into execution. I knew all about the tripwires and man-traps, for it was common talk round here, and on my way up the drive I cut them with a pair of scissors that I had taken with me for that purpose. I had no idea that Vaizey had chosen the same night to pay me another visit. I arrived at The Priory and found, as I expected, that the house was in darkness. With the aid of a ladder from the tool-shed I got into the library.

'When I first saw the safe I believed that I had taken all my trouble for nothing, but to my surprise I found that it was unlocked. I concluded that Vaizey had been in a hurry for some reason or other, and had closed the door but had forgotten to turn the key. I found the letters I was seeking in the safe, together with several other documents compromising a number of people whose names are well-known throughout the land, and I made a bonfire of the lot in the grate. I burnt every paper I could lay my hands on, and had just finished when I heard someone knock loudly on the front door.'

'That must have been me,' put in Bill.

'Yes,' said the colonel, nodding. 'I didn't know that at the time, of course. I made a quick exit down the ladder and hastened home as fast as I could. While I was undressing, I discovered that one of my cufflinks was missing. I had barely got to bed when the phone message came telling me that Iris had been taken ill at

The Priory. I was astounded, for I fully believed that she was in bed and asleep.'

'Of course,' said Bill, 'she recognised the cufflink as yours, and knowing that you had been there, probably concluded that you were also guilty of the murder. I think it would be as well if you acquainted her with the facts of Trevor's confession at once. It will relieve her mind.'

'I'll do so now,' agreed the colonel. 'You might as well come with me.'

Bill was so delighted at the proposal of seeing Iris that he was on his feet in a flash, a fact which caused Bluey considerable amusement. Leaving the reporter in the study, he followed Wells across the landing to a door on the opposite side.

The colonel pushed it softly open and entered. Bill, waiting outside with ill-concealed impatience, heard him say something in a low voice, and presently he came to the door and beckoned him inside.

It was a daintily furnished bedroom, and in the large white-painted bed lay Iris. Her face was very pale, and around her eyes were deep purple circles. She gave Bill a wan smile as he approached the bedside. 'I'm glad you're better, Miss Wells,' he said gently, looking down at the white face upturned to his. 'I have good news for you, I think.'

He briefly informed her of Robert Trevor's confession, and as he continued her eyes brightened, and a faint splash of colour crept into her pale cheeks.

'Oh, you don't know what a relief it is to me,' she murmured when he concluded.

'I think I can guess,' said Bill with a smile. 'You thought it was your father who killed Vaizey, didn't you?'

She nodded, and slowly in a faltering voice that grew stronger as she proceeded, related what had happened on the night of Milton Vaizey's death.

She had seen her father go out, and guessing his intention had followed him, but had lost him in the darkness of the wood. She had lingered about in the clearing, undecided whether to go on to The Priory or return home. Then she had seen Vaizey approaching, and when Trevor had sprung out of the bushes and fired the fatal shot, she had believed that it was her father, for she had been able only to dimly make out his figure and they were both of the same build. Her suspicion had been confirmed, she believed, when Bill had found the broken cufflink. The shock had proved too much for her overstrained nerves, and she had collapsed.

Looking into Bill's eyes as she concluded her faltering story, she saw the expression of admiration that he was unable to conceal, and her colour deepened. 'I hated you that night in the wood,' she said suddenly.

'I know you did,' said Bill. 'I hated myself. But I couldn't do anything else.'

'You were rather a dear though, really,' she murmured. 'I'm glad it was you and — and not Inspector Browne.'

'Not nearly so glad as I am!' said Bill Groom heartily.

★ ★ ★

'And that's the last mystery solved,' remarked Bill a few minutes later as he and Bluey sped towards London. 'It has been a very pretty problem, and I must say I wouldn't have missed it for anything,' he said with emphasis, his thoughts fixed on the occupant of a certain room at The Beeches.

'I'm still in the dark as to how you worked it all out,' replied Bluey.

'Brains, old man — sheer brains!' answered his friend as he successfully negotiated a sharp bend. 'You might not have noticed it, but I bristle with them. I was convinced almost from the first that Miss Bingham's death was an accident; therefore it was Vaizey whom the murderer had intended to kill. It was obvious, too, that Vaizey knew this, and that was the reason for the fear under which he seemed to have been living for some time. I admit that until he was himself killed, and we found the letter from The Ghost in his pocket, I never suspected the truth. But when I came to think it out, it seemed to me absurd to think that Vaizey, if it was The Ghost he was afraid of, would have put himself in the other's power by going to meet him at such a place and such a late hour. I looked at the case from every angle, and I saw at once that supposing Vaizey himself was The Ghost, a lot of things were immediately made clear. I accordingly adopted that view as a working hypothesis.'

'But it was all pure speculation,' objected Bluey.

'No, you're wrong, old man,' answered Bill. 'It was ordinary inductive reasoning, which is employed in all scientific research. I started with the purely tentative theory that Milton Vaizey and The Ghost were one and the same. I adopted it as a proposition that was worth testing, and I accordingly tested it with each fact in my possession. As each fact said 'Yes', and not a single fact said 'No', its probability increased rapidly by a sort of geometrical progression. If Vaizey was The Ghost, it struck me that the person who had been responsible for his murder was most likely to have been one of his victims or one of their relations, and that the possible motive might be that of revenge.

'I remembered the photograph that I had seen on Trevor's writing table on my first visit, and wondered if he could possibly be connected with the affair. Miss Bingham had been killed by someone who was undoubtedly an expert in the use of a rifle, and a remarkably good shot. Two people came instantly under suspicion in my mind — Colonel Wells and Robert Trevor; for both of them, in their various professions, would of necessity be expert in the use of firearms.

'When I looked through the list of all the suicides during the past two years at the Yard, I suddenly came upon the name of Trevor. A young man living in a flat in Piccadilly named Chris Trevor, the son of Robert Trevor, the explorer, had shot himself for apparently no reason. My suspicions were strengthened, and then it flashed on me how I could prove that Trevor was the man who killed Miss Bingham at least, and as I was certain the same hand was also responsible for the murder of Vaizey, the person who was guilty of both crimes.

'I remembered the shred of leather covered with blood which the murderer had left on the barbed-wire fence while escaping. That blood should provide me with an invisible clue that would show once and for all whether or not it was Trevor. He had said that during his visits to central Africa he had contracted relapsing fever. Now, the germs that cause relapsing fever are clearly discernible under the microscope in the blood of the person who is subject to it. I accordingly went to Sir Bryan Walsh, who searched for and found them. My case against Trevor was complete. I also had a fairly clear idea as to Colonel Wells's connection with the affair, once I was certain that Vaizey was The Ghost.

'I had learned that the way through Boulter's Wood led only to The Beeches, and therefore it seemed feasible to suppose that the letter found by Vaizey was going to be delivered at the colonel's house. If this were so, then The Ghost was obviously blackmailing Wells. The only reason that could have made Iris faint at the sight of the cufflink was, I felt sure, because she knew the owner; and since the colonel was almost certainly in the clutches of the Ghost, and The Ghost was Milton Vaizey, I concluded that the reason for her agitation was because she thought her father was the murderer. And there you are!'

'It sounds perfectly simple, now that it's explained,' said Bluey as they drew up at Bill's flat. 'You're a marvel at the game, old man.'

'Come in and have a smoke,' said Bill in reply.

'I say — ' began Bluey when they reached the sitting room, but a wave of Bill's hand silenced him. Crossing to the telephone, Bill took off the receiver and asked for an Esher number.

'What on earth are you going to do now?' demanded Bluey in amazement.

'Shut up!' said Bill tersely. He turned again to the phone. 'Is that Colonel Wells?' he queried. 'Please put me through to Miss Wells's room.' His quick eye had noted the instrument by her bedside that morning. 'Is that you, Miss — er — Iris?' he asked.

There was a slight hesitation, and a soft voice answered: 'Yes. Who is that?'

'Groom,' he said. 'Er — Bill Groom. I shall — er — be near Esher this weekend. Do you think I might call and — and — er — enquire after your health?'

Over the telephone came a faint ripple of laughter. 'I was wondering if you'd ring up,' said Iris.

'Oh, were you?' Bill's voice was elated. 'There's a chance I may be in Esher this — this afternoon, and — er — and — ' He broke off. There was a short silence, and then:

'Couldn't you make it a certainty?' she said softly.

GRIM DEATH
MURDER IN MANUSCRIPT
THE GLASS ARROW
THE THIRD KEY
THE ROYAL FLUSH MURDERS
THE SQUEALER
MR. WHIPPLE EXPLAINS
THE SEVEN CLUES
THE CHAINED MAN
THE HOUSE OF THE GOAT
THE FOOTBALL POOL MURDERS
THE HAND OF FEAR
SORCERER'S HOUSE
THE HANGMAN
THE CON MAN
MISTER BIG
THE JOCKEY
THE SILVER HORSESHOE
THE TUDOR GARDEN MYSTERY
THE SHOW MUST GO ON
SINISTER HOUSE
THE WITCHES' MOON